KARIN BOYE (1900-1941) was a Swedish poet and author of novels and short stories, publishing her first collection of poems at age 22. She also worked as a literary critic, journalist, and translator from German. As a public intellectual, Boye promoted the placement of literature and art in the political sphere, whether early in her life as an active member of the Clarté movement or later as a member of Samfundet De Nio, a literary society that promoted peace and women's issues through Swedish literature. In 1931, Boye co-founded the avant-garde journal *Spektrum* in which she would publish her translation (with Erik Mesterton) of T.S. Eliot's 'The Wasteland', a moment seen as bringing literary modernism to Sweden. Toward the end of her life she was an active pacifist. Her dystopian novel, *Kallocain*, published in 1940, foreshadows World War II in its depiction of a totalitarian state. In 1941, Boye took her life.

AMANDA DOXTATER is Barbro Osher Endowed Chair of Swedish Studies at the University of Washington where she specializes in Swedish Literature and Nordic Cinema. Her research interests include: the intersections between melodrama and modernism; representations of childhood and the family in the Nordic welfare state; issues of class, race and ethnicity in Swedish cinema; translation studies; and public-facing humanities. *Crisis* is the first work she has translated for publication.

Some other books from Norvik Press

Johan Borgen: *Little Lord* (translated by Janet Garton)

Kerstin Ekman: *City of Light* (translated by Linda Schenck)

Kerstin Ekman: *The Angel House* (translated by Sarah Death)

Kerstin Ekman: *The Spring* (translated by Linda Schenck)

Kerstin Ekman: *Witches' Rings* (translated by Linda Schenck)

Vigdis Hjorth: *A House in Norway* (translated by Charlotte Barslund)

Sigurd Hoel: *A Fortnight Before the Frost* (translated by Sverre Lyngstad)

Svava Jakobsdóttir: *Gunnlöth's Tale* (translated by Oliver Watts)

Selma Lagerlöf: *Mårbacka* (translated by Sarah Death)

Selma Lagerlöf: *The Emperor of Portugallia* (translated by Peter Graves)

Hagar Olsson: *Chitambo* (translated by Sarah Death)

Klaus Rifbjerg: *Terminal Innocence* (translated by Paul Larkin)

Edith Södergran: *The Poet Who Created Herself: Selected Letters of Edith Södergran* (translated by Silvester Mazzarella)

Kirsten Thorup: *The God of Chance* (translated by Janet Garton)

Dorrit Willumsen: *Bang: A Novel about the Danish Writer* (translated by Marina Allemano)

Crisis

by

Karin Boye

Translated from the Swedish
and with an
Introduction by Amanda Doxtater

Norvik Press
2020

Originally published as *Kris* in 1934.

This translation and afterword © Amanda Doxtater 2020.
The translator's moral right to be identified as the translator of the work has been asserted.

Norvik Press Series B: English Translations of Scandinavian Literature, no. 74

A catalogue record for this book is available from the British Library.

ISBN: 978-1-909408-35-7

Norvik Press
Department of Scandinavian Studies
UCL
Gower Street
London WC1E 6BT
United Kingdom
Website: www.norvikpress.com
E-mail address: norvik.press@ucl.ac.uk

Managing editors: Elettra Carbone, Sarah Death, Janet Garton, C. Claire Thomson.

Layout: Essi Viitanen
Cover image: *The apples of New York* (1905). New York Botanical Garden, LuEsther T. Mertz Library.

This translation was supported by a grant from the Anglo-Swedish Literary Foundation.

This publication was made possible by the generous support of Barbro Osher and her commitment to promoting Swedish education, culture and arts.

This translation is dedicated to Helena Forsås-Scott in gratitude for her years of scholarship on Nordic women writers, and for trusting me to bring *Crisis* into English.

Contents

Introduction 9
Amanda Doxtater

CRISIS..21

Translator's Afterword 181
Amanda Doxtater

Bibliography..187

Introduction

Crisis epitomizes Swedish author Karin Boye's (1900-1941) capacity to write in a way that is queer, cerebral, imaginative, moving, sometimes formally estranging, occasionally tedious, and above all, wild. Her brilliance lies in her ability to conjure up the schematic, gendered distinctions between feeling and thinking, drawing on the force of traditional oppositions — irrational/rational, subconscious/conscious, black/white, male/female — to then throw them into disarray. Boye's prose can produce electric, prickly sensations akin to the pleasures of reading an author like Clarice Lispector. Her writing generates emotion that rattles the shields of the gods, flinging reason into the abyss. This force is inextricable from a painfully meticulous and occasionally pedantic intellect that picks everything apart, taking pleasure in analysis that never seems to end. Translating *Crisis* involved conveying these disparate registers simultaneously: Karin Boye the intellectual who is at home (and, I suppose, just as existentially unsettled) analyzing the work of T. S. Eliot, articulating the ways in which language both limits and forms our experience of the world, winding her prose together so tightly that readers must pry their way through it line by intricately-tangled line. And also Boye the hyperbolic stylist, whose feeling for the dramatic manifests itself in audacious, sweeping passages at once intimate and irreverently fantastical. *Crisis* is a deluge of emotional intellectualism.

Over the years, critics have written about Boye using approaches that variously remove her from the historical and political time in which she lived or tie her closely to it. Margit Abenius, who knew Boye during their university days at

Uppsala, wrote the first biography of Boye, *Drabbad av renhet* (Afflicted by Purity) in 1950 and later edited her collected works. Abenius portrays Boye as something between a pure, sensitive, imp-like poetess yearning to flee into a romantic world of interior experience and a delicate, depressive poet shattered by the horrors of two world wars. By contrast, Gunilla Dommelöf's ground-breaking work in the 1980s secured Boye's place in the Swedish canon not only as a poet, but also as a cultural critic and journalist very much engaged in the cultural-political world in which she lived. Here Boye emerges as a resilient feminist and literary intellectual who brought high modernism to Sweden. Critics have taken Boye's fascination with psychology in different directions as well. Barbro Gustafsson Rosenqvist reads Boye as engaged with contemporary theories of depth psychology that circulated during her lifetime, while Peter Jansson reads *Crisis* through the universal lens of mortality. In his literary portrait of Boye, Crister Enander paints her as an anti-capitalist, anti-fascist critic with almost revolutionary sensibilities. And Johan Svedjedal's 600-page literary biography of Boye, *Den nya dagen gryr: Karin Boyes författarliv* (2017) (A New Day Dawns: The Literary Life of Karin Boye) casts new light on the complicated ways that Boye's personal life was imbricated in her literary and political life, as a woman having complicated desires and complicated relationships with both women and men, and as a member of the intellectual avant-garde in Sweden in the 1930s. There is something irresistible about imagining how Boye's work relates to her individual experience and her capacity for self-observation. As Enander writes, 'Karin Boye's complex personality has captivated many. But she's also an exception. Few Swedish poets can claim Boye's well-developed interplay between intellectual analysis and the more chaotic realities of emotional life. Over and again, in shifting circumstances and situations of crisis, Boye is able to take a distancing step back and, as if from a distance, observe herself.'[1]

---

[1] 'Karin Boyes komplexa personlighet har fängslat många. Så är hon också ett undantag. Få svenska poeter har som Boye ett så väl utvecklat samspel mellan intellektuell analys och känslolivets mer kaotiska verklighet. Om och

Introduction

As the novel in Boye's *oeuvre* that most explicitly presents itself as 'autobiographical,' *Crisis* (*Kris*, 1934) lends itself readily to such imaginings. Boye wrote *Crisis* after returning from an extended stay of about eight months in Berlin in 1932-33, during which she experienced first-hand the Weimar Republic as it drew its last breaths. The Nazi party grew stronger, and Berlin was an awful admixture of unemployment and misery, with Jews being accosted in the streets. But during the same period, Boye underwent a very productive series of psychoanalytic sessions that allowed her to stop trying to cure her 'inversion' and to take advantage of the relative sexual freedom that Weimar Berlin offered her to live openly as a lesbian. Psychoanalysis also provided Boye with the tools to write *Crisis*. The novel re-stages events that Boye experienced fourteen years earlier as a precocious, devout twenty-year-old woman attending a year-long course in Stockholm at a teachers' college for women. Ostensibly, *Crisis* illuminates the work of self-analysis for Boye and her pseudo-autobiographical protagonist Malin Forst by depicting concrete individual experience: depression, the paralysis of will, feeling inadequate or helpless in a world that desperately needs help, and then an intense infatuation with a classmate that reorients everything.

The powers of analysis that Boye levels at her former self can be unrelenting. Throughout the book's various staged encounters, Boye subjects Malin again and again to choruses of onlookers who judge and measure her from various angles. The critique of Malin's awkwardness that Boye delivers via the catty letters of her frenemy classmates, to give one example, is heart-wrenching. These subtle moments in *Crisis* suggest the dark shadows Boye dealt with throughout her life and make the reader feel their presence. Boye's suicide at age forty-one has often served as the dominant framework through which to read her life and writing, but while it is important

---

om igen, i skiftande skeenden och krislägen i sitt liv, förmår Boye att ta ett distanserande steg bakåt och liksom på avstånd betrakta sig själv.' (Crister Enander, *Relief: författarporträtt*, p. 271) All translations from Swedish are my own.

to acknowledge Boye's fascination with the death drive, this should not overshadow the force of life that surges alongside it through the novel.

This streak of optimism shines forth in Erik Mesterton's review of *Crisis* in *The Anglo-Swedish Review* in December 1934 when he describes Boye's novel as telling a universal tale of individual development and enlightenment. *Crisis*, he writes, 'traces [Malin's] progress from orthodox religion, with the spiritual conflict and sense of guilt which it produced, to a mystical intuition of the sensuous beauty and creative mystery of the universe. The profound change in her most intimate perceptions and feelings and her essential attitude is made concrete in, and at the same time symbolised by, her understanding of the physical beauty of another girl and its spiritual significance. The profundity of the theme, and the fearlessness and spiritual grace of the author's mind, have produced a book which is unique in Swedish literature.'[2] What sets *Crisis* apart from the other contemporary Swedish novels of that year, Mesterton argues, is precisely its focus on life as a 'sense of life as growth and aspiration' in contrast to the other works that conveyed a general 'sense of decline.' That the novel has been reprinted multiple times in Swedish, most recently in 2017, provides a sense not only of the novel's canonical status but also of the way that generations continue to appreciate its uniqueness.

To call the novel autobiographical is, ultimately, to diminish the extent to which Boye uses her own biography to raise universal questions that transcend the individual self. Malin's personal crisis is fundamentally an existential crisis of faith. At age twenty, her ability to relinquish her will to God's, something that had always come easily to her and provided great solace, suddenly becomes impossible. Religion no longer offers sufficient explanation for the persistence of human suffering in the world and Malin's aspirations to a kind of will-less martyrdom fail to calm her as well. Instead, the guilt she feels at having herself escaped experiencing human atrocity

---

[2] Written in English. (Mesterton, *Speglingar*, p. 70-71)

engulfs her. Beyond a strictly religious crisis, the book raises numerous questions about what might be called the human condition: Why do humans continue to inflict suffering on one another? By what ethical and moral codes shall we build our societies and our world, and what role does the individual play in this endeavor? Central to Malin's crisis is the question of how much free will individuals actually hold in the face of institutions, ideologies, and the pressures of socialization. *Crisis* also asks fundamental questions about what it might mean to belong, to desire, to love, and to obsess.

Boye's literary figuration of actual events in her life often takes on a titillating life of its own, whether as an encounter between the scraggly figure of Satan and a motley conglomeration of saints and martyrs on high, or when a one-celled protozoan organism struck by the oceanic infatuation of the cosmos instigates a synesthetic dialogue among the senses: sight, hearing, touch and taste. The performative energy of Boye's self-imagination, in other words, is dizzying. Her crisis can telescope out into vast mythical or metaphysical planes: as a struggle between black and white, Dionysian and Apollonian, or down into the molecular specificity of the gooey, primeval moment when a flailing, pitiful embryo is thrust painfully, reluctantly into life. The radical negotiation of scale in *Crisis*, one of its defining characteristics, speaks to the scope of Boye's ambition with the novel. In a single work, she illuminates the tiniest corners of a young woman's psyche in order to grapple with universal questions about life and suffering.

Crucially, *Crisis* also reflects the anxieties and upheavals of the historical moment between the two world wars in which it was written. Boye was among the many artists and intellectuals at the time for whom the incomprehensible devastation of WWI called into question the inherent stability of traditional values and institutions. *Crisis* consequently upends the credibility not only of religious institutions but also of the slew of social institutions that had previously grounded Malin's worldview. In one remarkable scene, Boye makes tenuous the authority of medical science when a socialite doctor dismisses Malin's anxiety and tears as the misguided worries of a young woman who is too focused on the world's problems. 'Don't worry your pretty little head about such things' is the essence of his patronizing advice. The institution of the bourgeois family doesn't fare much better. Although Boye reverses the gender roles that she actually experienced when she paints Malin's father as a tyrannical patriarch and her mother as utterly submissive to his will (growing up, Boye's mother Signe was more domineering), the egregious imbalance of power between them shatters any hope of harmony brought about through traditional, bourgeois domesticity. And perhaps most pronounced is Boye's questioning of pedagogical institutions in the novel. As a young student studying to become a teacher, Malin's religious crisis is inextricable from her disillusionment with the educational system in which she is immersed. The religious and moral instruction she receives in order to instruct the next tender generation is revealed again and again as brutally prohibiting students from embracing life and the project of their own edification.

Although Boye didn't identify as a political revolutionary, her work was deeply invested in ideas about individual and social transformation that circulated at the time under the term cultural radicalism (*kulturradikalismen*). She was a public intellectual and, in the 1930s especially, a member of a small, elite group of writers, visual artists, architects, educators, social and city planners on the left who were reading Freud and Marx together to imagine a new kind of human being (*den nya människan*) and a new form of society. Boye's intellectual circle was deeply enmeshed in the creation of the Swedish welfare state. In 1931, with author and editor Josef Riwkin, Boye co-founded the avant-garde journal and later publishing house *Spektrum*, which went on to publish a variety of texts and visual art exploring the intersection of the individual with the political, social, and the aesthetic. In his study of the *Spektrum* collective, Johan Svedjedal depicts Boye as 'an incisive critic on the left, ironic, biting, fearless and irreverent, a thoughtful observer who saw through male-dominated society and capitalism.'[3] Not unlike the configuration of intellectual discussions in *Crisis*, *Spektrum* drew together a diverse array of conversations on literature, architecture, public policy, psychoanalysis, and visual art. Modernist poets including Vilhelm Ekelund and Elmer Diktonius were published alongside psychologists and social scientists like Anna Freud, Erich Fromm, Wilhelm Reich, and social engineers, urban planners, and architects such as Gunnar Myrdal and Sven Markelius. Boye left the avant-garde group around 1933 as she left for Berlin, partly to extricate herself from the tangle of Bohemian sexual experimentation and promiscuous love affairs that accompanied *Spektrum*.

It was in *Spektrum* that Boye and Erik Mesterton published their translation of T. S. Eliot's poem 'The Wasteland' into Swedish in 1932, a moment that is often considered to have brought literary modernism to Sweden. Or rather, it opened the Anglophone and continental floodgates; Finnish-Swedish authors like Elmer Diktonius, Edith Södergran and Hagar Olsson had already been working in that mode for several years. It's no coincidence that *Crisis*, which comes into the world two years after 'The Wasteland' appears in Swedish, bears the marks of this interwar, European movement. *Crisis* and *Spektrum* each reflect modernism's sometimes utopian optimism that from the wake of immense destruction or crisis one could rebuild. If only psychology and art could allow individuals deeper insight into their inner psyches and if enough people undertook such a project of self-knowledge, a new, egalitarian society might emerge.

Crisis exemplifies an attempt to reimagine society by attending to a crisis in aesthetic form. Underlying the novel as a modernist literary experiment is Boye's sense that language as a system has ceased functioning either as a reliable source of meaning or as a means of representing reality. Both Boye and Malin fantasize about experiencing the world without or beyond the distorting influence of language. We see this in the

---

[3] 'en skarp vänsterskribent, ironisk, rapp, orädd och fräck, en genomtänkt genomskådare av manssamhället och kapitalismen.' (Johan Svedjedal, *Spektrum: den svenska drömmen*, p. 31)

scene in the novel in which Malin visits her former mentor. In an almost mystical encounter, the objects surrounding her in the apartment reveal themselves to her as distinct from the words that describe them: cup, chair, shelf. Of course Boye has no choice but to avail herself of language to write a novel — it's the modernist's dilemma to have to employ an inherited and imperfect system of representation in order to destroy or renew it. Part of what makes *Crisis* so challenging is that the work is trying to reveal language itself as inherently challenging, malleable and imperfect.

Boye's solution is to dramatize the breaking of rules. For instance, when the powers play chess, competing for control of Malin's fate, Boye very deliberately has black make the first move. She needs this to happen — in defiance of the rules of chess in which white always starts — so that in her metaphysical battle for existence, black's Dionysian powers of dissolution and chaos upstage white's Apollonian powers to impose rules and keep everything together. Likewise, intentional mistakes — the number of inhabitants she places in Nineveh differs from the number in the Bible, for instance — expose that for a modernist author breaking the rules elegantly reveals the shortcomings of representation itself.

As a translator, conveying Boye's very palpable intention to compose a highly experimental narrative entailed tapping into a swirling, fomenting desire — the energy she felt couldn't be contained by any traditional, linear narrative — as well as into the desire to harness the resulting fragments of text as they flew out in every direction. Boye's experimentation with form in *Crisis* is not always easy to read and almost nothing about it is easy to translate; its edges are hard. There are few (if any) moments when Boye reaches out to lead her reader in. The novel provides little in the way of explanatory guidance to orient us in the world of Malin's experience. Instead we are left to observe the written traces of its workings. While we are privy to the debate about Malin's consciousness, it is not always easy to identify with it. Stylistically, it doesn't resemble 'typical' modernist prose like Virginia Woolf's stream of consciousness. The novel's most interesting formal innovation happens not at the level of flowing sentences, but at the level of interlinking paragraphs and sections. While rhythms definitely emerge from the interaction and juxtaposition of scenes in *Crisis*, the overall effect is to produce something more like a compounding sensibility, or modernist effect through accumulation. The typesetting of the 1934 first edition in particular punctuates scenes visually with blank space. Some sections begin at the bottom or middle of a page, others at the top, as if echoing Boye's often jagged alternation between voices and registers. At the same time, like the blank wall that Malin gazes up at in the novel's opening scene, these voids between sections of text allow the reader a momentary reprieve from the intensity of their prose.

Boye remains a fascinating figure in part because the personal struggles she treats in *Crisis* still resonate in contemporary discussions about how the personal and political are or might be imbricated. For Boye, this imbrication entailed contributing to the creation of public life by aesthetic means. Although Boye is perhaps still best known, at least in Sweden, as a poet, she also wrote several novels and short stories, published newspaper articles of literary and cultural critique and also supported herself as a translator at times. Boye's prose allows her readers to watch her act out this conflict between yearning to retreat into a universe of personal aesthetic experience and yearning (or perhaps feeling obligated) to contribute to the world around her through political action. The tension between political or social engagement on the one hand and the personal and private-psychological was extremely productive for Boye, in particular with *Crisis*. While Boye never resolves this tension, I like to believe that the gently mystical and very queer scenes in the book in which Malin senses — whether by catching a glance or by feeling the presence of a stranger in the crowd — that she is both fundamentally herself and someone entirely different at the very same time, part of a new, organic community, show that Boye hasn't given up trying.

Perhaps Boye's most crucial contribution with *Crisis* is the book's varied investment in desire — queer and otherwise.

Amanda Doxtater

Desire assumes many different forms throughout the novel, from Malin's initial attempts to unify her will in God to the painful longing she will feel for her classmate, Siv. Siv embodies an irreverent form of enlightenment— she couldn't care a lick what others think of her—but she also represents the kind of intense bodily desire that makes you feel naked through your clothes. Turning Siv into the symbol for a way of being in the world, or displacing desire onto an eternal battle of white vs. black, or even back in time onto your former self, raises interesting questions about the extent to which Boye felt compelled to downplay the lesbianism in the novel by encoding it as something impersonal or abstract. In that respect, *Crisis* stands as an immensely creative repression or sublimation of desire. Contemporary critics, not eager (or perhaps not able) to acknowledge the homosexuality in the book overtly, elevated Siv as the embodiment of a new kind of Christianity, spirituality, or superior moral force in the world. With this translation I have tried to capture the delicate intellectualism and voluptuous feelings of this queer love as well as the transfixing way that Siv conveys something both profound and elegantly sweet. I've attempted to translate desire in this novel such that *Crisis* may be counted as the masterpiece of queer, inter-war modernism that I believe it to be.

CRISIS

She sat once again to pray in the assembly hall of the teachers' college at the start of another school year. Would it be as full, as suffused and overflowing with vitality as the previous one? She had no doubt. She might encounter sorrow and suffering, but such superficial things would be blown away like dust in eternal winds. Peace. Not as the world giveth.

Slowly the benches filled with primary school children and student teachers from the teachers' college. Malin let her eyes glide along the wall. The large, bright hall with its paintings by Hjortzberg made a deep impression on her every time.

Pious images and symbols encircling the walls like a wreath. Holy, venerable symbols, which had been chiseled into expressions of exalted truths thousands of years ago. Each century imbued these truths with the new warmth of new life and the new meaning of new experience, until the symbols bound the believers of all eras together into a fellowship spanning centuries. Mighty, inexhaustible symbols, to which generation upon generation would come, immersing themselves as if at a well, drawing forth new treasures time and time again.

The nails and the crown of thorns: martyrdom awaits each and every person who truly yields to His will. The holy martyrs of the church are innumerable. Even more are they who silently bear their cross, never to be counted among the saints. They who, far beyond the bounds of the church, committed their sacrifice to a divine fire that compelled them against their will. 'I can of mine own self do nothing,' man says. And God compels him. Strength such as he never before conceived unfurls like wings. The nails and the crown of thorns: nothing the least bit beautiful in reality, nothing romantic, nothing before which anyone would bow. Yet together on the wall, they become an ornament, a stylized jewel. But at its most truthful. For that is its inner essence: an ethereal jewel. Who will not want to wear it in the final moment, when the call is heard? The most exalted of honors.

The pelican, which nourishes its young with its own blood: redemption. A redemption taking place every day, at every moment, everywhere; for the one who suffers is God eternal. He suffers with us in our suffering, through His own instruments, with His instruments, so that He may win and bless those over whom He has yet to gain power. In this way God's kingdom slowly triumphs.

And the chalice. The same yet again. 'This is my blood, shed for thee.' A peculiar fellowship, that we are *able* to sacrifice for each another, take each other's place, bear each other's burdens, reap what others have sown, as we in turn sow for others. A terrifying fellowship that extends across the world of humankind. We subsist on the death of others, on animals and plants that lay down their lives. Then we too die and relinquish our atoms to become the matter of new life — in this way life flows endlessly back into life. Shouldn't it also be thus in the realm of the spirit? A living being — a single wave in a vast, ongoing undulation — receiving sacrifice and offering sacrifice, nothing in and of itself, everything in its devotion to the One, who is, who was, and who shall be.

Over there, the ship on the sea ... Could it be Jonah's ship? The wonderful tale of the meek and all-too-human Jonah, he too an instrument of God for all his weakness. Altogether too small to comprehend the Lord's pity for Nineveh, that great city of ten thousand inhabitants, none of whom could discern between their right hand and their left 'and also much cattle.' That is how we instruments are, too meager to discern the thoughts of the Eternal One. And yet His instruments still.

Like glimmering gold, the symbols sank through her resting and waiting soul. Brimming with significance and continuity, endless in their multiplicity, enveloping the material objects of this life with reverent reminders, one by one. Reminders that, despite their shifting forms, always gave nourishment to the same single and eternal aspiration: the absorption of human will into that of God.

The wall directly before her had been left plain, undecorated, and after the engrossing images along the others, she found respite in the naked simplicity of its whiteness. It brought her back to a dream she'd had the previous autumn.

She was walking through an immense church. The light cascaded through the dusky colors of stained-glass windows. Countless varieties of sculptures and paintings adorned the nave and aisles. 'This is the temple that people of every epoch come to build,' said the famous historian of religion who was guiding her around. Looking eagerly around the room, she was struck dumb with admiration, though looking at the many colors and shapes made her eyes ache a little. 'But all of this,' her guide continued, 'culminates in the Mysterium Magnum. See how simple things are here.' They had entered a passageway with a low, wooden ceiling and whitewashed walls. No decorations, no ornamentation, just a calming white light that filled the room, perfectly bright yet gentle enough not to dazzle her. A great relief after the throng of images of the other room. 'What is the Mysterium Magnum?' she asked, but received no answer. She could feel herself on the verge of waking and, fearing that she might never learn the answer to this enigma, she began to shout over and over, 'What is the Mysterium Magnum? What is the Mysterium Magnum?' And then, as she awoke, she heard the answer, though she couldn't say whether it came from her guide, from a voice above, or from within herself: *'It is when the life of a human being becomes the life of God.'*

Seeing the bare white wall before her reminded her of that dream. The ultimate objective was actually so simple, so unaffectedly simple: not my own will, but Thine. The obliteration of individual will, so that only God's will be done; emptiness to make space for fullness. Malin bowed her head and prayed, in devotion, in submission, the prayer she always prayed, to the Holy Spirit.

Kurtn Boye

Never anything else. Most often wordlessly.

At first it required effort. To collect herself, to devote herself utterly to concentration, to rap at a door or make her way farther and farther down a long road, through primeval forests, feeling her way, crossing lusterless seas, forging a route along rugged paths, through thickets. Then, suddenly, she *arrived*. Into peace. The immense peace would flow through her entire being, through her soul, but also through the veins of her body, coursing out to the very tips of her fingers. Filled as she was, embraced by peace and blessedness, it was no longer a struggle to remain collected, without fragmentation, without fear. Nothing was difficult any longer; no temptations remained. Then she was equipped to venture into the world without being of the world, to go forth as a vessel and instrument of God. She simply *could not* treat an unkind remark with unkindness. Such pain passed straight through her — sharp as a sword — but without inciting resistance, without arousing hate or wrath, for there was no longer any cause to recoil in selfish anguish. No longer *could* she judge others or rise against any injustice; for what could injustice matter to someone who has utterly renounced her self? All that was possible was to judge herself, for not having strength to overcome and transform everything she encountered with love, or rather with God's love pulsing within her. There was no longer any indolence, her feet went where they were meant to go of their own accord, and had the command come to ascend the pyre, she would have obeyed, without struggle or hesitation, simply because she willed what God willed. God expressed His will through man's relinquished soul. This was the state of which Meister Eckhart spoke when he said that it was a greater thing to step over a stone in such a state of mind than to accomplish prodigious deeds in any other.

Malin had come to realize that it took at most twenty minutes of struggle and exertion to achieve that peace and the complete resignation of her will. She had only to collect herself. Like Jacob: 'I will not let thee go, except Thou bless me.' She prayed copiously. It was her greatest joy. But always for the Holy Spirit, never for anything else.

When her best friend, defying all expectation, succeeded in passing her exams and graduating, the Principal had come up to Malin, taken her hand and said, 'Our prayers have been answered, dear child!' Malin had stared at her, puzzled. Was Fröken Dalén actually implying that Malin had prayed for Netta to receive her diploma? That would have been sacrilege. She had remained silent, however, as it didn't seem the appropriate moment to discuss such matters. Or had she held her tongue out of cowardice and laziness? It tormented her to pluck upon the fragile strings of her inner self in front of others but nonetheless she did usually speak up and confess, with the deep blush of shyness. Of course she was a coward, of course she was lazy. That was precisely why her greatest wish was to disappear, to dissolve into air, air through which sunlight passed. Even if she went astray, everything would be made whole and pure by fully submitting her will to be sacrificed once again.

And the autumn that had just passed, that wonderful autumn ... She had gone about her work at the teachers' college, and she could still say, 'Yet not I ...' Without the least resistance or rebellion, she had allowed all animosity, both there and at home, to pass through her like a sword from God. The ecstasies she had occasionally experienced during the previous year had culminated in one single, complete, unbroken submission. 'Nevertheless I live, yet not I...'

Previously there had been eclipses, the desert drought of which all mystics speak, when the springs of the soul seem to run dry and no rain falls from Heaven. But she had waited, knowing well that it was also an evil temptation to desire inner happiness and wealth instead of doing God's will in the desert as well as in a tropical spring. She had waited, and now it had passed. She had desired nothing else but to be shaped into God's obedient instrument, and her wish had been granted.

Karin Boye

What could possibly befall her now?

'He who the world in Thee hath found, hath conquered all with joy unbound.'

This was Malin Forst, age twenty.

Dialogue I: On Sound Ideals

Crisis

DOCTOR. No, illness is illness! Why should we regard neurasthenia as if it were any different from tonsillitis? On that front, I really have got past all of the prejudice.

THEOLOGIAN. If that's the case, it's a prejudice I would gladly go back to. Frankly, the difference between the two seems enormous to me. You can use strictly scientific criteria to draw a line between having tonsillitis and not having tonsillitis — either you find this or that bacterium in your blood, or some unhealthy change or other to the organ, or some such thing — or you don't. But using scientific observation to try and draw a line between a mind that's healthy and one that's unwell? That line will always be more or less arbitrary. I mean, of course, apart from obvious cases of delusion.

DOCTOR. No need to take it as far as delusion, even. As soon as someone becomes at all problematic to deal with, there's bound to be something the matter.

HUMANIST. There you go again! That, surely, is an arbitrary standard to impose! It's too simplistic to test for something like a neurosis bacterium. No, we have to rely on something much more elusive: the social interactions and habits of the person in question. Those vary according to time and place and social class, as we know, turning into social norms that depend entirely on the taste and interests of whoever's doing the judging!

THEOLOGIAN. Though you're putting it a bit too starkly, I meant something along those lines as well. Norms aren't determined by nature; there's no biological norm to speak of at least. Norms are created by and only by humans — on

Karin Boye

that much we agree. Human existence has brought something entirely new into the Creation, something that can't be subjected to biological suppositions. This life of the spirit is completely new and has its own unique laws and objectives. Your 'social' norms, on the other hand, seem to me to be just as crudely superficial as those derived from biology. Social norms can only be seen from the outside and never illuminate any higher, spiritual existence.

DOCTOR. Just what exactly do you hope to achieve by spouting on about your esoteric enigmas? Forgive me for speaking bluntly — but I don't think you're being entirely impartial in your thinking. I suspect you're giving a little nod to the long history of your own institution, establishing this higher, spiritual life as the norm simply to bolster the reputations of a whole slew of great neurotics who might not look so impressive if held up to medical standards.

THEOLOGIAN. Well, of course! A nod, as you call it! I fully admit to having 'biases,' which you find so repulsive. You couldn't be more wrong to think I'd be ashamed of them. I'm willing to doubt everything from science to multiplication tables — everything, except what it is that gives life its worth. Don't lecture me with your worn-out platitudes about 'life lies' from back when an intellectualistic view of life was *en vogue*. This case isn't a question of some distorted interpretation of facts, but rather about a specific valuation of facts themselves, and consequently has nothing to do with being 'true' or 'false' in any intellectual sense. In other words: yes, it's true that millions of people have *known* their personal God deep within themselves, in His story, in His messengers, and most clearly and incomparably in the Son of Man. When we look at historical figures in this light, it becomes clear just how irrelevant our modern, hygienic foolishness is when it comes to answering fundamental questions. What does it matter if God's most devoted followers occasionally let their piety be expressed in a way you would be inclined to call pathological — perhaps I would as well, in as much as I, too, am imprisoned within the prejudices of our own age. We approach such things with a different set of values than

Crisis

they do, lower values, ones that have yet to be tested. You call Luther a neurotic — I call him a genius and spiritually fit as a fiddle. I can also tell you that his scale of values, and that of other Christians before and after him, was a *sound* scale, for it emanated from the experience of those who had attained the highest and seen the farthest. This modern, secular scale of values, on the other hand, is *unsound* because it passes judgment from beneath, seeing the highest of all spiritual phenomena from the worm's-eye view of someone spiritually undeveloped — note that I say *spiritually* undeveloped, not necessarily intellectually.

HUMANIST. It's all well and good that your values derive from strong and direct experience of the world. But how can you insist that it's impossible for us heathens to have experienced the same thing, but with completely different nuances and gradations? How can you believe, in other words, that everyone else is wrong and only you are right? As if it even makes sense to speak of right and wrong when it comes to the question of values? I despise the lot of you crude moralizers, because you confuse two fundamentally distinct categories of things. The first category is your private, inner aesthetic experiences — and I readily admit, of course, that these are what illuminate life and make it vibrant. Yet such experiences also vary from one individual to the next. The second category is what I would call *ethics*, namely certain rules to govern our actions — note that I'm talking about our actions, not our thoughts or feelings. Ethics keep us from devouring each other entirely. The less we mix aesthetics and ethics the better. When you think about it, isn't it criminal to stunt and terrify and contort what's most fragile within us — that which can only unfold voluntarily, like a fragile blossom? By this I mean our inner ethical (or if you prefer, our inner aesthetic, our inner hygienic) capacity to choose, our subtle, spiritual power to love — everything you would stunt and terrify and contort with *commandments*? And another thing, it's unfathomably stupid to mix your version of private aesthetics into everything having to do with the way societies function. I'm thinking mostly of laws, but also of other forms of education. We should strive to provide citizens with the smoothest and least conspicuous defense mechanisms possible in order to live a good life — and avoid mindlessly creating everything in the image of your aesthetic imperatives!

THEOLOGIAN. As much *laisser-aller* as possible, you mean! I admit, that's a bit too lax for me. Imagine the practical consequences for a moment: you're standing in front of a group of children — where do you imagine leading them? What will you give the young people standing before you with their insatiable hunger for ideals? Will you toss them stones of indifference instead of handing them the bread of life? Leave them to grope through the darkness on their own? No. Let me say it again: We must begin from the highest point, not the lowest — and most importantly, not have nothingness as our point of departure.

HUMANIST. If man needs ideals, you can be sure he'll find them on his own!

THEOLOGIAN. But what kind of ideals can he find, without any guidance? Surely only gruesomely primitive ones.

HUMANIST. At least no ideals that are arbitrarily tacked onto us.

DOCTOR. Frankly, I think you two are being a bit abstract. As far as I'm concerned, the best thing would be to return to the so-called worm's-eye view, by which I mean empirical facts, always solid ground to stand on. In the grand scheme of things my experience might not seem vast, but this much I can tell you: I know those mental patients I've treated much better than any great figures in legends. Not only am I familiar with what they claim to be themselves and with the ideals they consciously live by, but with numerous other perspectives and dimensions as well. I know the murky places they refuse to acknowledge, but which exist nevertheless. I see how patients inhabit those places, creating their own monsters that dwell and flourish despite every exertion of their will. It *is* conceivable, and not entirely unlikely, that their ideals were too constrictive from the outset, and when those ideals couldn't accommodate enough of their internal

energy, that energy necessarily sets up its own residence —
to the detriment of its neighbors. If that's true, I would be
more than willing to label such ideals *unsound*, at least for the
person in question. Perhaps the same goes for all of us — we
seem to be created more alike than not, after all. Your saintly
legends also have a fair amount to say on this subject. Show
me the saint who bore sainthood without also enduring their
own private little hell, worse than any ordinary mortal could
endure! But show me them from the inside, not gilded as in
the legends! They'd look a bit different then, I'd imagine. Less
enviable!

THEOLOGIAN. Enviable! Yes, well, less enviable from the
perspective of your happy-go-lucky notion that good deeds
will result in happiness, perhaps, but you still fathom nothing
of their reward! Incidentally, the idea that all believers have
such a difficult time of it is untrue, to put it mildly. I would
even go so far as to claim that a person who, from your point
of view, is nothing but a pitiable neurotic, when seen from a
higher, spiritual plane, might have reached a more noble state
of health than your supposedly sound eating-and-sleeping
machines who run around dispensing their sound reason and
natural instincts. I pity the poor child who has never taken
part in spiritual life — even with all the anguish it entails —
for neither will he ever know what it is to be delivered from
that anguish.

HUMANIST. I really can't fathom how it would be any more
sound to overstrain yourself emotionally than it would be to
delude yourself, for example, that you're a bird and can fly.
Doesn't it all end the same way? Life contradicts us — facts
give us a big red X in the margin.

THEOLOGIAN. Nor did I say anything about overstraining
yourself. I just said that basing moral value on the likelihood
that doing good acts will make people happy is fundamentally
a bad ethical system; we shouldn't be scared of ordeals and
suffering. Gold is purified in fire and in 'the mystery of
struggle and pain' and that is the last thing we should be
ungrateful for. No, no one with faith as a grain of mustard
seed need worry about overexertion. Quite the opposite, I

believe that many of the current residents of our mental hospitals would never have fallen victim to their 'illnesses' — which probably just began as malice or idleness or some other inclination toward vice — had they acquired the simple habit of saying their morning prayers every day, seriously and in earnest. Then they could have resisted external and internal turmoil in a different way, armed with more than just this world to support them. Sure, they would have met with obstacles and temptation, they would have struggled and suffered, of course, but they might have prevailed. This perfectly exemplifies the dire consequences of your biological methods of observation! It's always easier — I mean in the beginning, naturally, because it inevitably ends terribly — to blame an 'illness' that you can't do anything about than to grapple, seriously and honestly, with the most difficult and stubborn malady of all — *sin*. And sin has one, and only one, guaranteed cure: forgiveness. But if you run away from *that*, and run instead to secular doctors and other quacks who claim to be able to heal your soul and assuage your feelings of sin and guilt, then you've sold your birthright for a stew of lentils. To say nothing of the fact that you've sold your soul.

DOCTOR. You don't actually know anything about that, you just believe it!

THEOLOGIAN. What I know, I know from experience. As if you, with all of your assertions and hypotheses, actually 'know' any more than I, or even as much!

DOCTOR. Working hypotheses! At least we *want* to pursue knowledge, but you, you don't want to know anything. You could care less about pursuing knowledge — you're already done — you just believe!

THEOLOGIAN. At least the foundations of our ethical choices are established and stable, which is more than science will ever be able to achieve! In addition, we search and struggle as well, and do so quite bitterly and intently, let me tell you! 'Just believe!' As if it were so simple! Our true 'knowledge' drifts with the breeze; tomorrow your edifice of learning will be replaced by another, which in turn will be torn down to make space for one that is even newer, more modern ...

Which reminds me of something that Hans Christian Andersen sagely remarked in one of his stories: 'In faith is everything; in our knowledge hardly anything!'

DOCTOR. Does he mean to suggest that his remark proves that faith is superior to knowledge?

THEOLOGIAN. It sounds like it!

HUMANIST. May I kindly point out that our discussion has now sunk to a very low level without either of you gentlemen noticing? As a matter of fact, it's as though we've digressed back to obsolete intellectual quandaries again. But isn't this lapse itself worth pondering? Is it really possible for values to endure unchanged, when facts continually put on a new face? I don't think so. I think values, too, are subject to change.

THEOLOGIAN. That's impossible. What I experience as values, no one can take away from me.

Silence, as all three descend into their own contemplations.

Karin Boye

What wrathful sovereign commands the clouds, when they gather their dark iron legions, encircle the sky, rattle their shields and set forth to plunder the light from the world?

O Lord, Lord, art even Thou mutable? How can Thy countenance in our soul darken and transform from one day to the next? How can the Father cast off his mantle of light and preside as a merciless Judge?

Thou canst not be kin, Lord, to man-made idols. They are monsters with the heads of beasts, crowned with the double diadem of terror and power. They glimmer in the darkness with green cat-eyes, they purr with all the cruelty that man sheds along the path. Thou canst not be reckoned among them, Lord, my Father!

But at the edge of the world, at the plunge into precipitous darkness, the thoughts of the living flicker like startled bats, rushing downward, blinded by night, stunned by the abyss, flapping above the steep slope, and hearing only the distant roar of foreign seas that rinse the roots of the conscious world.

From the depths, a wind or a breath or an exhalation rises, someone beginning to move. It's enough to make the abyss reverberate with thunder and blaze with lightning. The bats flee, shrieking and whimpering. Along the mountain walls the shadows of immensity quiver.

What do we know of the Dreadful One!

Crisis

The Powers Play Chess.

The game extends in all directions. The exertions of the two adversaries traverse space like taut threads of lightning, billions of minutely shifting combinations emerge and are annihilated in the blink of an eye. Problems are displaced, distorted, combined, with innumerable solutions and innumerable impediments. The gaze seeks out just one of the battling opponents, just one square of the millions at play and even this proves more than the human eye can bear.

BLACK opens the match. The first move is always sheathed in darkness and mystery. No one knows what possibilities surge from the gnarl of creation. A new life is begotten from single-celled proto-organisms and must then traverse the long chain of evolution into the human. Through its pre-historic slumber the growing being must repeat fantastic transformations, repeat the initial bracing and the mighty leap, repeat the tensed configuration of forces out of which life hurls itself into new, daring adaptions, repeating the centuries' rolling Mississippi of creation compressed into the rapids of Imatra in nine months. Nine months...? Perhaps each embryo actually journeys through all the ages of time. At the beginning of every life a dark eternity gapes.

WHITE answers with a move equally mysterious. An unknown anguish presses upon the being, blocking it like an impenetrable cliff-face, forcing it into other, still viable channels. It follows the fluctuating forms and their constant obstacles until it is left panting as if pursued, whether crashing down in wild experiment or atrophying in impotent degeneration. What prehistoric dreams of resistance and fear stir in the embryo's cells, as it is driven from one form into another, only to be forced the next instant to abandon its previous self yet again? That suction of ocean currents as they carry the unresisting proto-creatures at once toward their demise and toward their life? That ice-age premonition of death in the cold blood of reptiles? That eternal inadequacy in the face of nature's erratic unpredictability and the tenacious weight of matter?

BLACK presses onward. A horde of shadowy, half-human figures jostle their way forward through the inception, trying to catch a glimpse of their own reflection in the future seed. Green-eyed ancestors, shaggy cave dwellers bare their gleaming teeth. Man, the greatest predator, has come into being, the species with weapons deadlier than the saber-toothed tiger and recklessness enough to develop them.

WHITE follows, makes a defensive move. Pressure grinds it from two directions. On one side: the immense forces abutting — the darkness of night, the cloudburst, the earthquake and the predatory animals forced into agonizing consciousness, agonizing reflection. On the other: the pressure of its own tribe, the proximity between human and human, forcing it into restraint, obedience, submission, privation. The eons, when order congealed, when commandments drank grandeur out of death and agony, when societies crystallized and stratified — does this all seep like a murky dream through that which is still coming into being? Or is it instead like a temperament, an inclination, a hard won tendency to flinch when the harsh voice speaks?

BLACK — cuts to the quick. The growing seed bursts out of its hull: birth. Brutal as a murderous crime of passion — rupture, blood, and pain.

WHITE retaliates with all its might. Strands of tissue tighten, contracting like a net around a gasping fish. Hurled toward an unknown world, on the verge of quickened consciousness, squeezed between blood and flesh in a spasm, until the organs that have only just begun to function must now fight for their lives... Anguish, eternal anguish, grips the scrabbling insect, driven through the vortex of birth.

Crisis

— — —

BLACK. I come from within, I run like primal fire through thousands of blood vessels, each as fine as a strand of hair, along the sensitive, well-developed pathways of nerves. With my hunger, a hunger which all the sumptuousness in the world could not satisfy, a still tightly-closed bud swells into a ravenous mouth, and I erupt into the two small, greedy paws of a wild beast, hot like flame, trembling in anticipation of the leap, ready to conquer the external world.

WHITE. I seek my weapons from outside, I seek anything to enclose your flame. And I find what I seek! Out there, among tangible, intimately desired objects, booms a voice, to which everything submits. It booms like a storm over grass. Nothing can withstand it. Blessedly merciful when it rewards you; cold, cold when it claims instant obedience. A metal voice, a nakedly slashing will, embodied in sound. It comes from above, filling the cosmos, itself caused by nothing and knowing no *why* other than: *because that is what I want.* A metallic ringing full of unuttered menace affords a glimpse of a vacant, dead universe in which love has died. From desolate ground abandoned fortresses rise, their portals locked, their windows only dead eyes; no one opens up for the forgotten child and out of the sky's acrid blue the earth's final autumn descends...

That voice is my most powerful piece, it moves far and wide, in every direction, assuming every role. With it I'll chase you from position to position, close in on you, strangle you.

BLACK. A captive beast scratches and bites. I summon the green-eyed ancestors from out of the depths, they sharpen their flint knives, they hiss their death spells.

WHITE. I'll capture your pieces and make them mine! She heeds the call of the outside world so intensely, and you imagine that this is to your advantage? She'll just hear THE VOICE all the more intensely. Scratch and bite? She'll tear herself apart. You're betting on those greedy hands? THE VOICE will quash them. Do you not hear the slow metallic ringing, *'Paws off! Look but don't touch!'* And hands fall limply away, powerless. The lives of these little hands begin a hibernation from which they dare not awaken. The hands of children rarely appear so lifeless. As if they neither dared nor cared to defend themselves against the attack, they let themselves be bitten by frost and dangle there, swollen violet clumps. An accident! says the fool — but I know the real cause of accidents.

BLACK. I retreat from these wilted hands. I retreat from the slumbering body. In you, mouth of the child, I remain awake. There my voracious fire still grasps at conquests. Come, beautiful words, and I shall grant you life as vital as that of any tangible thing! I create a world twin to the one we see, a world of secrets and delight.

WHITE. A world of isolation that will never truly resemble the real one! Where is its certitude to be found? Where is its powerful, streaming contact with others? — In the world of reality she remains silent. Yes, the good child all parents wish for: silent, amiable, obedient.

BLACK. You don't know my ways. Dreams wild as nightmares! Secret desires and fantasies, full of rage and pleasure, dreams she would never dare repeat to an adult...

WHITE. *THE VOICE* extends even into dreams. *THE VOICE* reaches deeper than dreams. Dreams shall die.

— — —

BLACK. Pain, blood, and anguish again! Only now a new turning point: adolescence. The ego expands to a Titan; defiance breaks its chains. What previously submitted, must now rear up in hatred!

WHITE. *THE VOICE* forbids hatred. Hatred is hideous.

BLACK. Guard your pieces well! Your voice can be rendered harmless. It can be degraded to that of a tyrannical father, against whom revolt becomes a duty. The young human gropes for new ideals with which to steady herself as she pries herself loose from the subjugation of childhood.

WHITE. I am protected. The ideal is there. The mother, ignorant of the world, resigned, not at all able to resist wickedness. Does she not respond to the commands of *THE VOICE* in precisely the same way? She retreats into the world of music. In the external world she obeys and serves, serves

Crisis

and obeys. She has submitted — she is good! Her presence emits a pale, passive love, but love nonetheless. What other choice is there but to admire and follow, to reach toward those silvery figures who wandered through the world never letting themselves be stained by their suffering? Those who were rewarded with the cross and the pyre, who with their last breath still humbly gave thanks while shrouding themselves in the silvery luster of self-denial — their cloak of victory? Those silvery figures will become her ideal. But do you realize whence the adamant resolve of their demands comes? Without command, no obedience. Without *THE VOICE*, none of self-denial's silvery luster. My most valuable piece remains in play and is devastating your back ranks!

BLACK. My embers are scarlet, my blaze white, and my flames flicker blue. The fires raging in her mind are burning too hot for you to extinguish them.

WHITE. Just subdue and encircle. Her days will be a struggle against forbidden feelings. At night she'll sleep on the floor to escape dreams she is not allowed to dream. You'll advance no farther!

BLACK. You're clever, as I've seen in a thousand matches before. Clever enough, but you'll still never defeat me. The closest you have come is an inglorious *remise* — the sound of a shot, or the splash of a body falling into the water, or the heavy breaths of one who sleeps and sleeps, never again to wake. Must I stoop to that level this time as well? I can glimpse that possibility even now... But not yet, not for a long while. Youth is tough; youth can withstand despair. I'll work in confluence with your plans and maneuver inward for the time being. I am the lightning, I am the storm that lays waste to mountains and forests. And should you block my path I'll become the earthquake that undermines the earth and shakes entire cities. The spirit of destruction? And self-destruction? That too. Call me what you like. I am everything that pummels and seizes, I am flame and desire, I am hatred and cruelty, I am the power of creation, it is I who dares leap. I am the spirit of action, ruinous and all-consuming, without which no foundation can be laid, no building erected. I am the

Karin Boye

core of the will. I am what drives everything forward. You are the obstruction holding everything back! You are the dogged No! If you block me I'll ravage inward. If you let me loose I'll raze the world! But if you smother me — I will call you death!

WHITE. I could call you death as well! If I released you, you couldn't raze the earth — it's much too dense — but drown it in a storm surge. And nor can you defeat me! The core of the will? It is I who am the core of the will. Only where I am found can you even begin to speak of a will. It may be that without you I am dead, but without me you are nothing but a formless tempest! The dogged No is one of the foundations essential to the cosmos and form. And between the two of us, borne up by our rivalry, life hovers...

What a match! In the beginning your position was so strong, and now... it's rare that I pin you this forcefully.

— — —

BLACK. I have forged a way through. I have made room! It came like the cracking of ice, I surge as in a black froth of stars. I am saved — life is saved!

All her fear, all her petrification shattered in one great ecstasy! It burst into bloom in broad daylight — love under her feet, love arching over her head, love in every direction, she breathed love — all fear dissolved with the blossoming of an immense desire.

WHITE. Whose love?

My plans are secret. I shall ensnare you.

BLACK. You don't scare me! A thousand times I'll pierce your guile and a thousand times more I'll place a new soul naked on a new shore!

WHITE. Defend yourself!

Crisis

The unease says to her: Get away! Always away!

What does it mean, this unease? Where does it lead? Driving one's soul to relinquish everything it has, hindering it from searching for anything new. What is this great weariness toward everything she has found, what is this great longing for something that no one can find that drives us to fold our hands in our lap — and despair?

It had always been this way. When she was little she would burst into tears whenever she even heard the word longing. The word was too strong, charged with a deadly power. It spoke to what had been *lost forever* — the ultimate, the only, which had sunk into the depths at the beginning of time, no one knows when. Everything that was truly beautiful could grip her with such a torment of hopeless longing that sometimes her whole body would rock back and forth as if in pain. Somewhere beyond, somewhere beyond...

Then again, she could recall one evening shortly after her conversion when she and her mother had stood on the porch gazing out at a transparently golden sky. She recalled the aspens, and how the fine leaves of each slender tree were silhouetted in black against the light. In that moment she became suddenly aware that her anxiety had stilled. Nothing drove her out and beyond, and in the presence of that moment she felt eternal peace blossoming within her. And again, in the last six months, as she had quieted herself in willing obedience, it had filled her as never before: the harbor in a storm, the repose that settles in after being torn asunder.

And now — — —

Karin Boye

She couldn't comprehend how it had happened. At Christmas she had still been calm. She remembered walking through the woods during the final days of her Christmas break, sprigs of lingonberry poked through thawing snow and the air smelled of moss and snowmelt, clean and wet. And peace, the only thing worth possessing, pervaded her. It was a peace beyond all comprehension. She walked and walked in the wet, fresh forest, at peace.

Something must have happened since then, for she had become someone else. But she couldn't think of anything.

The anxiety was there again, as never before.

Somehow she had lost her connection with divine will.

Longing is like playing. When it turns serious they call it anguish.

Away! Always away! Away! Away!

Crisis

Pray and work!

Textbooks lay in piles on her desk. One had been lying open at the same page for quite some time. How long had she been sitting over her pedagogy assignment? It was impossible to finish. She read a single paragraph in the middle of the left page again and again without having the least clue what it meant. The letters slid meaninglessly in a long row that she couldn't decipher, as if they had been hurled into immateriality by the force of a mystical centrifuge. And at the center of this surging vortex sat a strange impatience that didn't know what it wanted. It flung everything apart, shattered her focus, and dispersed concepts and thoughts like chaff in the wind. The resulting emptiness it left was filled only with itself, an impatience devoid of any purpose...

She got up and fell to her knees by her bed. Prayer! The only thing that would help. Only prayer could put her back together again, make her whole, and show her the way into the core of her being. But she couldn't pray. It must have been at least a week since she had been calm enough to immerse herself in prayer. That strange impatience stood in the way. It had to be overcome. It simply required the will to find a way.

'Nothing but my own laziness, my deficient willingness can hinder me,' she thought, closing her eyes.

But she couldn't sustain it. Over and again that peculiar anxiety split her, rearranged her insides, shattered her focus. She tried to collect herself, but it descended upon her like a compulsion, stronger than her will. She composed herself once more, but the very next moment her thoughts began to wander again and she wondered why it was so difficult to breathe and why she so longed to leap up and get away from there.

There was no point in trying to continue. Something stood in her way, something stronger than she.

A trial? You undergo a trial knowing that some expanse will open up on the other side.

Enduring a trial means continuing to live as if you could avail yourself of all the comfort and help that you so bitterly miss. And would that really be so hard when you know that, no matter what, God exists? When you know that everything is just a test?

But this time was different. *Then*, though she had been aware of being tested, her will had been whole and she had simply submitted to what she had no power over. Now the obstacle lay in her own will. In her deficient will.

Not a trial, in other words, but rather the evil that separated her from God.

What had she done? Of what was she guilty? How could she atone?

She shut her eyes again and with a painful exertion attempted to charge the closed door. If any cry into the darkness might reach the throne of God then hers would now — now — now — — —

But anxiety bound her in impotence, exploding her concentration from within. It filtered down, coating the objects around her like a fine dust, as she stared, unmoving, at the bright, glowing green lampshade, as if it might hold within it a way to flee, an escape. Slowly, slowly an unknown danger encroached, lacing itself around her throat.

Crisis

Pray and work!

If you can't pray — work!

And if I can't work?

Paralysis from head to toe. Paralysis of the soul. Paralysis of the will. And behind this paralysis a smoldering restlessness, which couldn't be expressed in movements, words, actions, thoughts — it just persisted there, consuming and draining her, day and night.

The worst of it was that she couldn't even collect herself enough to work. Neither homework nor class preparation could hold her focus — it was as if all her interest had been captured and melted down in the white-hot oven of anguish that burned deep inside her — with no hope of escape.

At the moment it was the third-grade history lesson she would be expected to give after break that had instigated her great despair: Birger Jarl and his sons. Time and again she tried convincing herself that she needn't let herself be pressed to the ground by something that she already knew, and which was a worldly matter that would soon be over anyway. Last autumn she had attended each class happily confident that no matter how badly things might go, she could at least do better the next time. Now every little thing filled her with despair. Perhaps not so much the fear that things would go wrong but rather her fear of the exertion needed to collect herself to accomplish anything. Do something, be something, will something. She had no strength for any of it.

Everything felt suffocatingly heavy and prolonged. The ultimate Demand was mightier than she. It reminded her of a nightmarish impression from her childhood: the sensation of

Karin Boye

something infinitely large that had to be conquered somehow — a mountainous loaf of bread that had to be bitten through, or a giant, slippery ball that had to be picked up without anything to grasp onto — or some other inexpressible, indescribable, incomprehensible thing that belonged to another world where different natural laws operated and which inevitably stirred feelings of desperate impotence in this world. She felt the same way now.

The very sight of the massive, heavy college doors in the morning was enough. Standing before them, she was assailed by an oppressive powerlessness, like Thumbelina at the foot of the giant's door, which she had to open despite her size. No, she would never manage such an immense exertion ... No, she didn't have the strength, she would have to wait until someone else lent a hand to help her... Still, day after day, she entered somehow.

Once inside, peering up at the wide stairway before her, she found her throat clenching again as if she were about to ascend a treacherous cliff face. No, she would never reach the top. And yet, day after day, she found herself standing in the classroom once more.

Every single morning felt like the beginning of a day that would be impossible to endure — heaping anguish to eat through like the pancake mountain a mile wide in the land of milk and honey. Strange as it may be, there's no expanse of time that doesn't eventually come to an end, and she would always find herself sitting on the train home at last. There she sat, nervous that she would miss her stop in Tullinge despite having made the same trip to and from school for six years. From the station it was a ten-minute walk, endless, endless to the foot of a hill. She would really have liked to sit down there and cry in despair. Though she hadn't ever done so and somehow always made it up the hill, by the time she arrived at the red house where she lived, it seemed to her as though a day in Hades lay behind her.

Not that the red house was the end of it either! New anguish, new despair awaited her there. Another afternoon consumed by endless hours drafting her lesson plans, then further hours of dread before anything got done. Immeasurable, unreasonable fear paralyzed and stifled her. With no time to complete a new version by morning she was forced to leave things as they were, though when she was done, she wanted nothing more than to rip up her pitiful results. Not that she even had the strength for such a violent act.

And then another night with new horrors.

What had she done to be hurled into the abyss like this? Somehow, she had failed. Everything she did now was just further failure to accomplish the task. At some point, there must have been a fork in the road, a point at which she still had options — and there she must have chosen evil. Now she no longer had any choice — she could no longer withstand the storm that had since taken possession of her from within. It had come howling in and carried her off, with no more concern for her thrashing than the sea has for a mosquito in its waves.

She couldn't say from where, precisely, or to whom, but her innermost self was pleading for help!

Unimaginable, that there would be none. No one has sinned so much that she can't be forgiven, granted her will is pure.

But that was the weak point.

Her will was impure! It was neither intact nor pure. She couldn't even gather herself to pray. She squirmed uneasily in her seat during her lessons, she scribbled and drew, her thoughts scattered in a thousand directions — her external thoughts, that is. Deep within her one thought remained immovable, and latched onto the only thing that filled her: anguish.

This is what they call *self-obsession* — something repulsive that you have to fight yourself clear of. Have to! But it's no use. This is what they call laxity that comes from having no will. Her will had been poisoned. By what people in the old days called the Devil? If so, then she was under the Devil's spell now.

And yet the very highest had once been lavished on her. She had glimpsed the realm of the eternal. She had made a sacred vow always, always to — — —

Karin Boye

'... and justly deserve Thy eternal damnation ...' Terrifying words. *Deserve* — an *eternal* — *damnation!*
YES!!

Even growing up she had known that life was terror. The accounts of the world war confirmed her intuition.

Then years passed and she forgot it. But now she knew it again to be true.

It came over her at night, after she went to bed. In the darkness it surfaced, bubbling up from reality's muddy depths. She saw everything with her own eyes and felt everything as if on her own body.

An old woman who had defended her village with weapons had been stripped naked by soldiers who then tied her to a gun carriage and dragged her behind it until literally nothing of her remained.

During the Finnish Revolution a family had their tongues nailed to the table...

At the storming of — dear God, dear God, spare me, I don't want to see that and yet I must — must I go through this again, and night after night?

She lay still, in a cold sweat, trying to chase away the horrific visions but failing. Think of something else? Impossible. Bloody human remains wherever she looked, and the fists of butchers extending their gleaming implements.

During the Thirty Years' War, one eyewitness recounts — — —

During the Middle Ages they used — — — this is how they did it — — —

The Inquisition — — —

She couldn't even groan, only see and feel.

In the past? So, then what? They were dead, tortured to death, but at peace? A sweet little thought. As if that might actually erase the reality of their suffering. As if the time

Karin Boye

of all times could actually *obliterate* an ounce of what had actually been. As if the forward march of time could ever *atone for* such limitless terror. *Then* it was real, *then* was their now: *then* held an eternity of suffering in the space of a second. That could never be undone. In one respect, everything existed, everything was real, both what had already occurred and what was happening now. That could never be changed. It was an established and unalterable fact best expressed in the dream of eternity: somewhere everything existed at once, all joy and all terror. Everything. But calling it God and Heaven at the same time meant considering that, in equal parts, it was also — the other. Taking consolation in the idea that something was in the past was as short-sighted as taking consolation in its being far away, as far away as in Södertälje...

She had forgotten this — and been happy!

> 'To feel joy, as siblings suffer,
> to rejoice in the chorus of millions despairing —
> sound the depths of hell, if you can,
> the depth of this sin you cannot reach.'

It was true! As was the peculiar way it continued:

> 'Christ sought to redeem joy,
> but joy embraced him not.
> Joy shall be strangled by terror
> and terror redeem the world.'

She repeated the last lines to herself in the dark and clung to them. They sounded like a promise. Was there some redemption *on the other side* of fear, upon draining the chalice of its last bitter dregs? After having tasted *everything* while showing neither doubt nor weakness? Perhaps over there, in that great eternity, something existed that was more than

Crisis

all joy and all fear. Perhaps some atonement might be found beyond the fear? Not because it was over — it wasn't — but *even though* it continued? A synthesis, a vertiginous Amen that could drown out even what was most horrific?

But surely not *that* — not accounts she had heard of the Thirty Years' War — — — ! Dear God, save me, make it all go away! — That was where her cowardice lay: in praying to be spared. To be spared everything that people not unlike her had actually gone through.

Even if it had been possible to escape thinking about it, did she believe it would be less real for that? 'It's so far away, as far away as Södertälje!' — Maybe we are all one over there, in eternity, perhaps that's why we must feel each other's pain, why it can't be avoided. From that same spring, unseen, unknown, yet present everywhere, came the feeling that she too must go through everything that others had, not like this, in her mind, lying snug in her own bed from which, no matter how great her anguish, she would still climb unharmed, though perhaps feeble from lack of sleep. No, in real life, in flesh and blood and nerves, in greater agony than the ghastliest of imaginations could conceive — in mutilation, an inestimable, inconceivable loss. Why should she escape it, when others hadn't been so fortunate? And *if* she escaped — all the worse! An unparalleled injustice, guilt altogether too great to bear. She had the most horrific insight: at the same time as realizing that atonement must lie beyond this suffering, beyond the sum of everything that had ever suffered in the world, a suffering with no remainder — she still resisted it, with all her might, didn't *wish* to be a part of it, didn't *wish* to receive it, *wished* to distance herself from that great, suffering mass, *wished* to evade it. Oh, couldn't there be even a tiny loophole by which to escape? Couldn't everything I endure in my imagination at least be deducted from the other, which is so much worse? Being submerged little by little into boiling oil, intestines slowly extracted from one's body? Some small installment paid on a debt that was due, the tiniest mitigation... Her cowardice was a mortal sin, that much she knew. Drawing back from all that humans were forced to suffer! Now and always and forever the only demand: 'not as I will, but as Thou wilt!'

And yet she could not.

Her life in God had been an illusion. Now that the great call had actually come, the call to relinquish her will completely, in complete devotion, she reneged. Or had she even had the strength to comply — before? If so, the fall must have occurred between then and now. Regardless — now she had fallen, irredeemably.

And know myself, therefore, to be worthy of eternal damnation.

At one point it crossed her mind that she might go speak with her confirmation priest, Reverend Borg. But the thought struck her as absurd. His confirmation lessons, though level-headed and practical, had actually spoken so little to her, and it had never occurred to her to seek him out to share her difficulties in the many years that had passed since then. His brisk manner and energetic bearing had always been enmeshed in the programmatic assurances of a religious official and this frightened her as something polished and lifeless, something painlessly inorganic, that never really came into contact with the existential struggles of the organic world. Just after her confirmation she had been able to predict his answers to questions, though the precise details of this escaped her now — no, there was nothing to gain by going to him. Eventually her thoughts settled upon her scripture teacher from the school's first- and second-year courses, Fröken Mogren.

The great advantage of talking with a regular teacher was that, rather than representing an institution, she was in a position to speak as her own person. Fröken Mogren seemed to a great degree to be her own person. She was middle-aged, large and heavy, with coarse features, which would have seemed heavy too had they not been tempered by a dreamy and attentive piousness. Her lessons were extremely eloquent, sometimes so much so that it could be difficult to get through the course, especially for the girls whose principal interests lay elsewhere. They dreaded these long scripture lessons and tried to hide their mighty yawns. But Malin listened, fascinated. It was a commentary on her own life that Fröken Mogren was imparting to those who had the

Karin Boye

ears to hear it. Everything was there, tinted and ennobled by her rich and fantastic personality, though not held together by any particularly strict coherence: childhood's completely disparate thoughts and feelings — the insecurity and searching of adolescence — the rich experiences of people and books that came with one's student years — and then the wide world of battling spirits, of religious movements, into all of which Fröken Mogren still, despite long years working through many books, travels, conferences, threw herself with the same great intensity that she had in her early youth, to be engulfed, always with the same helplessness and the same passion, by the bewildering whirl.

It was to her Malin wished to go: she wouldn't simply offer her some polished system, or point her towards some definitive path — yet she would undoubtedly have a great deal to share, her own experiences, exciting summaries of religious biographies, perhaps new and surprising perspectives.

After calling to make sure Fröken Mogren would be home, Malin traveled into Stockholm on a Sunday. It was an immense undertaking. She herself didn't fully comprehend how she had summoned the necessary resolve.

Her heart was pounding as she entered. She felt ashamed at the thought of demanding that someone else pay attention to her own self-centered concerns; concerns that moreover would probably be unpleasant to listen to. Her mortification only grew when she was met with a warm-heartedness that seemed to verge on a kind of gratitude. Fröken Mogren was sincerely grateful. The confidence that Malin showed in her, reaching out like that, out of the blue, to discuss something that had to be important, clearly meant a lot to her. Malin felt only embarrassment in the face of such cordiality.

It was almost impossible to know how to begin. Well — what should she say? What did she want to ask about? Things were what they were; there didn't seem to be anything to ask about at all.

Fröken Mogren coaxed her.

'Well,' she said, a bit shy and awkward herself. 'I understand, you know, that there's something in particular you've come all this way to talk about. I also know, of course, how terribly difficult it can be to come out with such things. And I can't say for sure that I'll even be of any help — what works for one person might not be right for someone else. But one can always listen. And I think, really, even that can be quite helpful. Sometimes it's easier to untangle a problem when someone else is listening. Isn't that so? And I'm always here to listen, if you ever want to tell me anything — it's the very least that we humans can do for one another — don't you think?'

'But even that is so much!' Malin said, and then fell silent again. She longed to blurt everything out all at once, but her question had neither beginning nor end and she herself had no idea where the knot lay.

Fröken Mogren lived on the top floor of an apartment building on the outskirts of the city. She had an extensive, if uninviting, view over black and red painted tin roofs with various sorts of chimneys and weathervanes and gutters, and far beneath, the impoverished, dreary streets covered in ankle-deep slush. Malin thought to herself that only a few months ago, all of this would have awakened longing and delight in her. It would have symbolized the kind of work Fröken Mogren had devoted herself to and which Malin dreamed of doing back then: serving among the city's children and youth. In addition to teaching at different high schools, Fröken Mogren did demanding volunteer work at a Christian Socialist night school, primarily for youth, all of which had aligned with Malin's own attitudes and future goals. Only a few months earlier, everything in this room would have spurred her aspirations — a simplicity verging on asceticism, with bookshelves the only thing that gestured toward personal property, and a view out over her calling: that dreary, impoverished part of the city. But now everything held only despair, even this place, which ought to have embodied her future and vocation, all because she lacked enough strength even to attempt mastering the tiniest fraction of such an enormous undertaking. Too heavy! Too big! Too overwhelming!

Still, she had to say something.

'I'm afraid that I'm dying a spiritual death,' she said feebly.

'My dear child, that sounds awful!' said Fröken Mogren, mild and motherly, and without the slightest hint of irony or condescension. 'What makes you think that?'

Once again Malin felt constricted, unable to articulate her thoughts.

'My will is evil,' she said, at last.

'I see,' said Fröken Mogren hesitantly, glancing at the floor. 'Yes, it's easy to believe that sometimes. So many people have believed the same thing, and even written doctrine around it. Saint Augustine, as you know, felt exactly that, so profoundly. Having been born and raised in a Lutheran country probably gives us unique insight into understanding his plight, and we can sympathize with him. Of course, it ultimately always varies from one person to the next, some are drawn to a happy and optimistic faith, while others must pass through darkness in order to come into the light. There are the once-born and then there are the twice-born, as William James puts it. What I'm trying to say is, let's take Luther as our primary example. He, as we know, was one who passed through darkness before coming into the light, and perhaps his faith became that much stronger and more unwavering because of it. I suspect that it might still be the case more often than not, that only after truly letting yourself take stock of all your weaknesses, every last one, can your eyes actually be opened to something new, something even more powerful.'

Malin sat listening, but the words made no particular impression on her. Saint Augustine and Luther had been able to endure their tribulations, but what did she have in common with them? A feeling of bitter envy toward those who had achieved salvation suddenly filled her — could there be a clearer sign that she was now truly abandoned? When hatred pervaded even her longing for salvation?

Fröken Mogren sensed that she hadn't really convinced her guest. Small wonder, really, considering that she had launched so quickly into church history and the psychology of religion.

The only thing to do, of course, was to start with Malin Forst herself, with her concrete problems.

'Perhaps you're having problems at home?' she asked in an uncertain voice.

Malin shook her head.

'No — yes — what I mean is, it's nothing like *that*. Or rather — you could say — that everything else is just a consequence of the other thing.'

'All right — — — what "other thing"?'

'I mean: the fact that I can't obey my own conscience. And that my conscience causes me so much pain, and that you can lose contact with God and then everything else spins out of control, at home and at the teachers' college, too, but none of that matters, because worst of all is the simple fact that I *cannot* obey — because I *do not want* to obey.'

Signe Mogren had no mind for abstraction. She despised everything to do with systems, and hated their futile attempts to trap the warm pulse of life within dead formulas. That said, she had an incredible memory for concrete, colorful facts — and to her, most facts were colorful. She also had an instinctive psychological sensibility that allowed her to see every person she met as another drama bubbling with life.

The fact that Malin preferred to express herself so abstractly sent Signe Mogren, flailing and clueless, into a flurry of speculation. As a woman working with the general public, she had at her disposal a rich gallery of people and fates to draw on. Out of the murky darkness of the street, in the sickly yellow light of the lamps, the faces emerged, each containing conflicting meanings, ill-matched features, and expressions contradicting one another. They glided before her mind's eye, clear images, this or that one lingering longer because it had occupied her more recently. There was, for example, a girl's young, soft, freckled face encircled by a mass of reddish hair, with a wide mouth that was so curiously unreliable... And yet that same unreliable mouth could smile warmly, unreservedly, more trustingly than anyone. For her, it was a matter of battling polygamous inclinations. Her fiancé would disappear again and again, staying away for months, giving her more than sufficient cause to suspect him of repeated infidelities, and yet she still couldn't resolve to leave him — the moment he was near her again, all was forgotten. But she also had difficulty confining herself exclusively to him... One man after the other would enter the picture; she was easily aroused and really did seem to love them all, each in their own way, faithfully even, as friends... She visited and unburdened herself of this, and eventually, as their conversation continued, it became apparent that her conscience was floundering. Deep down, her conscience knew she probably ought to limit herself to one and give up the others. But it was so difficult. Yet her conscience knew...

Would she be victorious and if so, when?

And another face: eyebrows knitted together over deep-set eyes, producing a bitter furrow down the middle of his forehead — but when the brows eased their grip the skin smoothed, revealing the clear forehead of a thinker, the forehead of a superior, if resigned, observer. A young worker who — though a communist, still enjoyed coming to talk with her — perhaps because he perceived in her some inner assurance — or maybe just because she was knowledgeable. He had read widely, including philosophy, but could nevertheless sometimes admit that the bitterness underlying revolution was a low and base feeling. But it was hard not to be bitter. He hadn't yet called it conscience — he hadn't come that far yet — but she knew that his conscience had begun its work, and she felt confident that one day he would acknowledge that as well.

She would very much like to see that day.

And a neck, a woman's neck, that at times supported a defiant toss of the head as if nothing weighed it down — though it was never more than pretend, when no one was there to observe it, it bent lower and lower beneath its invisible burden — the invisible burden of a child that had been on its way but had not been permitted to come into the world. The woman was proud, and Signe Mogren admired her. She was hewn of superb hardwood: resilient and dignified, even when her pride turned to arrogance. Her pride inhibited her from succumbing

Crisis

to her regret, but it remained nevertheless, in her neck when she wasn't thinking about it. The battle she was waging was a difficult one — but what timber would not yield when the Almighty forced her down His path, through the narrow doorway named remorse, and prayers of forgiveness! Signe Mogren was not one to instigate such battles of conscience. She knew God's mills to grind slowly, but precisely. She wished only to be present to assist when needed. Signe Mogren would keep a watchful eye on the woman with the proud soul; she expected glorious things from her afterwards.

She watched numerous other images glide past: alcoholics and prostitutes, ruthless men and vengeful women, young people flung between a carefree life of pleasure and asking the fundamental questions of life's purpose and meaning. They all carried within them a tenacious and inexorable spark of light: their conscience. It struck her as both strange and remarkable that each and every one of these people was just as capable of uttering Malin Forst's words — Malin had expressed herself *so* abstractly that, in effect, she had articulated the conflict at the heart of Christianity.

She couldn't help trying to convey as much:

'I find it so curious! Of course, I can't know exactly what it's like to walk in your shoes — but what you say applies to everyone, more or less. I can't help imagining that all Christians everywhere in the world, at this very moment, are engaged in precisely the same struggle — such an immense thought. And it's not just now, these questions have always existed, as long as the voice of God has been heard in man, much farther back than our chronology reaches — and they'll continue to exist in the future as well — they're eternal. Isn't that a frightfully immense thought? To my mind, all we can do is embrace this age-old struggle with new energy remembering that no one has been spared, not one of those we admire and wish to follow — not even *He* was spared from exactly the same battle: choosing between a conscience that taught him his Father's will, and his own will, that must inevitably surrender, even if he was the Son himself. Remember the wonderfully beautiful writing about

Karin Boye

Gethsemane — I'm referring to what happened afterward: "and angels came and ministered unto him." It's just such a glorious image of what is to be gained by having a clear conscience. Reading such things, it's impossible to fathom how anyone would resist what we know is in our best interest, at any rate not resist as tenaciously or for as long as we do...'

A tiny drop of sweat appeared at Malin's temple. She sat there thinking about all the things one was supposed to be willing to do. About everything that had happened during the Albigensian Crusades...

'I can't!' slipped from her mouth. But as if the expression itself held within it some rebellious defiance she had distorted to her own advantage, she anxiously substituted, 'I don't want to!' — and then crumpled under the pangs of her conscience.

Fröken Mogren's imagination fluttered immediately to the family tragedies and unharmonious homes from which children fled, whether justly or unjustly — then again, perhaps Malin simply had an unusual calling, perhaps even an imagined calling — Missionary work in Africa? Or ministering to the poor here in Sweden? Perhaps that was why she had sought her out specifically? Had something along these lines instigated her break with relatives and friends?

She sighed.

'I realize that I probably won't be of much help,' she said. 'But don't you think that you might feel even a little better if you tell me what's really bothering you?'

'I suppose,' said Malin, sounding unconvinced. At any rate, she had a feeling that if you started with A you should continue on to B. She collected herself.

'I think — often — about all of the evil that people have inflicted on one another. Then I think, why shouldn't I suffer like that too? Why should I be spared the ordeals that others have been through? At the very least, I should be *willing* to suffer, if it's God's will. But I'm not. And because I'm not willing — — — then — — — maybe it sounds dumb, but it's true — — — I deserve eternal — — — damnation — — —'

Though these last words were barely whispered, a look of horror spread instantly across Fröken Mogren's face. As she

Crisis

sat there quietly considering what to say next, her initial alarm seemed to transform into stern disapproval that bordered on indignation. She, who was accustomed to seeing people suffer as a result of actual, tangible sins, sensed that Malin was toying with grave matters.

'We *cannot* think like that, she said admonishingly. We *cannot* imagine that we have been abandoned by God. That's what Luther refers to when he talks about despondency, despair, and other *grave sins and vices.* He calls it sin and vice outright. We simply *must* purge such thoughts from our minds — — not pay them any heed — not even glance in their direction!'

'But it's my conscience we're talking about!'

'No, no, no it's not your conscience! Absolutely not, we can't think like that! You're wrong, you're mistaking your beliefs about conscience for true conscience!'

'In that case, how can *anyone* know what true conscience is? It's something you feel inside you, right!? Why should my conscience be of a different sort than anyone else's? If you can't trust your own conscience, what in the world can you trust!?'

'First of all, your conscience would never be that unreasonable! What you're saying is misguided nervousness and above all irrational, inhuman almost!'

Eagerly and incisively, as if praying for her very life, Malin defended her conscience:

'But it's not the least bit irrational! No more irrational than Christianity itself! Even if it were, it would still be higher than anything we'd call rational! Of course, it's true, as you just said, Fröken Mogren: that this struggle lies at the heart of Christendom itself! After all, which of the commandments is most important? Precisely: "*And thou shalt love the Lord thy God with all thy heart, and with all thy soul, and with all thy mind!*" Love fully, not halfway, and not by making little exceptions for this or that when it becomes more than you can bear! Doesn't the whole Sermon on the Mount also demand that we show our utter devotion to God rather than just obey individual commandments? Isn't that the one true requirement? But I, I

Karin Boye

can't! Because my will is lacking! I'm committing the greatest sin of all: turning away from God. I grieve the Holy Spirit!'

Fröken Mogren's indignation dissipated as quickly as it had appeared. For a second Malin's lofty words, more suited to mighty prophets, had startled her. Yet before her sat only a callow, highly-strung girl.

'I still think you should stop dwelling on such thoughts!' she said.

'Don't you think I haven't tried!? But there's no escaping your conscience. And really, *should* it be possible to escape?'

'Pray to God that He help you avoid such thoughts.'

'How would He help me avoid my own conscience?! And I can't pray for that.'

Fröken Mogren sat quietly, once again at a loss. What could she possibly say to make such a foolish child give up such nonsense? Perhaps engaging her in some practical work would divert her — ? The idea collapsed under the weight of its own implausibility: when you're completing a one-year teaching course, live out of town, and travel back and forth every day — you have neither time nor energy to devote to youth work in night school.

Nonetheless — her illusions must be replaced by something real. A thought struck Signe Mogren like an epiphany: what the child sitting before her needed was to have her eyes opened to the *truly* dangerous implications of her thinking — perhaps then a voice of true conscience, one to cure her of her fruitless rumination, would replace these illusory pangs of conscience.

'Something occurred to me just now that I have to tell you,' she said softly, and Malin lifted her head, listening.

'So, when you think about it, isn't it as much a temptation to let our thoughts continually revolve around our own paltry selves all the time? Isn't it equally arrogant to go around engrossed in yourself, or worse, thinking only about saving your own soul? Doing so will eventually leave you completely blind to anything but yourself, to all of your fellow human beings who are so much worse off in every way...'

Malin's eyes filled with anguish.

'But I haven't forgotten that!' she shot out. 'That's exactly what makes it so terrible!'

'What I mean,' Fröken Mogren replied quickly, 'is that we have so much to be thankful for, but we're so quick to forget that. It's simply not *right* to let thoughts about damnation or sinning against the Holy Spirit get a foothold in your soul. We *must* resist them. As Geijer wrote: '*Sorrow is sin, for the essence of existence is bliss.*' We ought to remind ourselves of that now and again, when we get the urge to obsess about our own insignificant selves... Oh, are you crying? Please don't cry, or on second thoughts, go right ahead and cry for a bit, I think you'll understand why, and every so often you'll look back on this moment as a reminder, and maybe doing so will eventually convince you that, despite everything, things are frightfully simple after all, more than you realized at the time, for it happens all the time, you know, that you encounter some problem that seems impossible to solve, you can't see any way through it, but then in the crucial moment, you realize that nothing was as difficult as you thought, and when push comes to shove, things resolve themselves and then you wonder how they ever looked so bleak, when there was no real danger at all, and when you finally find the path you're meant to take you're grateful for having had to confront such difficulty, and perhaps you're even happy that it seemed so immense and so difficult, because otherwise you might never have found your way — — — or at least I've frequently found, both in regard to myself and those who have confided in me, that so often it's the difficult times that no one would want to have missed, because you learn the most from them and ultimately, they're never more than a person can bear and endure — — — My dear girl, what kind of a friend would I be to leave you in this state. It simply wouldn't do to let you go sobbing into the street! Then again, why shouldn't that be allowed, after all, why are we so concerned with outward appearances? We shouldn't pay them any heed... At the very least remember Geijer, even if I haven't been able to help you with anything else, we can always keep his words in mind — — —'

When someone says *that's a shame!* — no matter how mildly —
what they really mean is *shame on you!*

And when they use the words *sin, vice,* what they mean is:
shame!

Saying *that's a shame!* to someone who is already ashamed
might well be meant as: 'There's no need to be ashamed!' —
but it will only make the person in question feel even more
ashamed: they were already ashamed, and now, they are also
ashamed of being ashamed.

Malin took little comfort in Geijer's comforting words: 'Sorrow
is sin, for the essence of existence is bliss.'

The words of the catechism offered scarcely more comfort:
'misbelief, despair and other great sin and vice.'

Sin piled upon sin in her growing sorrow; vice upon vice
increased her despair.

Crisis

(Excerpt of a letter from class member Dagny Ritzelius of the same teacher training course to a former schoolmate.)

— — — *Morality* can be quite peculiar sometimes, for instance: what could be so immoral about wearing a black velvet ribbon across your forehead? Is it because it's modern? Three girls in class have taken to wearing them, you know, as in old Renaissance paintings, and I have to admit, that although on Mia Lund it is too ghastly, the style suits the other two fairly well. Regardless of that, it could hardly be considered a question of *morality* — although the Principal turned it into one by taking time out of our scripture lesson to deal with the issue. We wouldn't interrupt class to address the question of what it is to be *unbecoming* (if that were an issue we'd never get around to learning any scripture in our class) — although the Principal's words did seem to suggest that wearing these ribbons was *unaesthetic*, which these days is how everyone preaches morality if they still want to seem refined. She put it something like this: 'Can't we agree that it's rather silly to make your hair look as strange as can be, particularly when it doesn't make you any more beautiful?' She made no mention of the velvet ribbons and nobody else said anything either, at first, not even the guilty ones. What objection would they have had to the general proposition that it was a silly thing to do etc. (see above)? Obviously, they wouldn't have worn velvet ribbons either if they hadn't thought that they looked good in them! The main issue, though, was that the Principal didn't like them. But at that moment a complete innocent piped up, her voice wavering on the verge of tears, to defend decorative

Karin Boye

coiffures in general! 'Certainly, it's the case — gulp,' she said, 'that trying to have a beautiful hairstyle doesn't make anyone more beautiful, gulp. (*Gulp* designates the sound of swallowing, as I'm sure you guessed.) But, gulp, wearing one's hair pulled back would be *hideous* — on some people that is,' she added wisely, because that's exactly how the Principal wears her hair, pulled back. (Malin Forst, who said this, couldn't be farther away from wearing velvet ribbons, quite the opposite, she has her hair in a pious bun at the base of her neck, parted down the middle and with window curtains over her ears. She dresses more conservatively than you'd expect of even the most prim and proper teacher!) 'Certainly no one could object to Fröken Forst's hairstyle,' the Principal said dryly, albeit with a hint of amusement in her voice, for the Principal does have a sense of humor, though not necessarily about herself, but I suppose that's really quite rare. Everyone sat there, more or less entertained, without saying anything; the Principal waited in vain for some voice of conscience from the real guilty parties. When the silence grew ridiculous, she sighed and said: 'Isn't that how it always goes. A lesson rolls like water off a duck's back to those meant to hear it, while others mistakenly take it to heart,' at which point she proceeded to talk about methodology in the gospels. I still like the Principal, she's very decent, and as I mentioned before, she has a sense of humor. Later, after the lesson, I asked Malin Forst if she really hadn't grasped that the Principal was referring to the velvet ribbons. No, she said, her eyes growing wide, it hadn't even occurred to her that it was about the *ribbons*! (Lord knows whether she had even noticed them, she's the kind of bookworm who's oblivious to everything.) But at some level Malin had known that the comment wasn't actually directed at her, she said, (looking all the while as though she was confessing to some mortal sin)! (!) 'But you were upset, of course,' I said, 'which is forgivable at the very least!' — 'Yes, *that* I was,' she said, 'but at one point I did also think that she might be referring to me — and I regret that so terribly much now, for it was fundamentally *dishonest* to think that! But I couldn't help myself! Why couldn't I help myself, can you explain that!?' — All of this is to say that Malin Forst is full of herself, and not a little hypocritical and above all, she's self-important and stuck-up. As far as I'm concerned, she can keep swallowing and gulping as long as she likes; it'll be good for her — I'm just afraid she's gulping out of anger rather than remorse. — — —

Karin Boye

(Excerpt of a letter from class member Rut Hellgren to her parents.)

— — — It's often the case that the spirit is far from what it should be. Many have yet to be clear about their chosen path. It happened in our class that a few girls took up dressing more as coquettes than as young teachers, at least in terms of their hair accessories. But then, they also received a well-deserved lecture from the Principal, and have since changed their appearance. Changing inwardly, though, may unfortunately not be so easy.

During the same incident, it also happened that someone pretended to be affected and seemed terribly upset about the Principal's 'injustice,' as if coming to their defense. I don't believe that it was just playacting, for she was almost crying with indignation. But what is it that motivates such people who basically sit in tense anticipation, ready to pounce greedily on accusations to defend themselves against? An unfounded desire to criticize, I imagine, on the part of people who are too cowardly actually to complain about a situation and cling instead to pretexts. There's a kernel of this in each of us every time we suffer some 'injury,' and we ought to reflect on that. It's quite repugnant. — — —

Crisis

(Excerpt from a diary written by Gertrud Wolmar, a class member.)

— — — I can't stop thinking about the unsettling event that happened today. I have to write about it in my diary.

There was a discussion in pedagogy, as there often is, and Malin Forst went on and on, as she so often does. There's something so extreme in her opinions, and that strikes me from the start as being in some way — improper! This time, as if forgetting where she was, she elegantly and persuasively asserted that our learning in school was essentially useless. (Of course, it was an exaggeration — it may not exactly be able to save our souls, but it's still worthwhile! But still, I'm sure that she believes what she's saying and despite what so many of our classmates think, she *doesn't* just say things to get on Professor Senander's good side.)

Anyway, Dagny Ritzelius went up to her afterward and said:

'You really do love giving lectures as if you were a professor, or something. Are you trying to show off your colossal intelligence? I can assure you that we're all very familiar with that already.'

(Dagny Ritzelius isn't stupid, but in this case she was completely wrong.)

It was almost unnerving to see Malin Forst's reaction: she stood with her head bowed down and her shoulders pressed together, like a hedgehog, and when she finally looked up at me she seemed about to burst into tears. She said: 'Sometimes all I want to do is throw myself on the floor and beg for everyone's forgiveness! — But that will never amount to

anything more than a fantasy, because, give in and *do* that —
and you're lost!'

Most unnerving was the *cunning* little grin on her face
when she said that last bit! It was forced, that much was clear,
naturally she had no reason to laugh, but it was as if she were
divulging her deepest life secrets — but do I care about her
secrets? — no, I can't even put it into words! Her words and
that smile made such a distressing impression on me, as
something sick, sick, sick — I felt like kicking and spitting on
her!

But, of course, that's no way to treat someone who's sick,
someone who deserves pity, and I was ashamed that such
thoughts even crossed my mind. Especially because Malin
Forst has her good sides, too. But I didn't judge myself too
harshly, that's how healthy people react to the sick. And of
course, I didn't actually need to kick and spit. But the whole
thing left me feeling so *disgusted*. At least I feel better knowing
that I was *right, biologically speaking*.

Or is it just that I don't like feeling sympathy? — — —

Crisis

No one knows from the outset who to call: my people. You're not born knowing, although you are said to be. Neither is it something you learn in school, though it might seem so. No, it's something you figure out as you make your way through life.

It's knowledge that's not easily grasped. Every now and then, amid the crowd, you glimpse a face that belongs to you... No, it's not the face exactly, but rather an event, a certain situation in which someone plays a particular role, a role that is my most inner and unique role, the role that, whether agonizing or pleasant, I've been born for and must endlessly repeat — and even without being exactly clear what it is about that role, I feel instinctively: yes, of course, that is me, standing over there — *it's so clearly us...* However scared or tranquil you might be, in that moment you experience an unbounded willingness to step into the breach and support this newly acquired, other I as naturally as supporting yourself; leaving yourself out in the cold would be unthinkable. No, it's more than a face! Magnificent faces can grip you with their purity or with the destiny etched in them, but they always remain 'them,' never 'us.' Anyone you encounter in *the role*, on the other hand, whether they be worthy of loathing or admiration, lays claim to every demand of friendship and you can deny them nothing. Tomorrow they may be a stranger again or perhaps even an enemy — but right now, as things stand in this moment, *it is us...*

It takes time to experience enough such encounters to apprehend them clearly. Understanding the watchword of your people, and comprehending what a struggle it is to be forced unconditionally into befriending the acquaintances of your friends. You notice that struggle every time but you can't comprehend it. The events that call forth such vital, substantial, and predestined fellowship may seem so ridiculous or inconsequential that you would prefer to avoid them altogether. And yet they are the small signs guiding you into greater currents.

Malin Forst, austere and despairing Malin Forst, didn't dwell on the question of why she had spoken up in the cause of those velvet ribbons — and with such rarely exhibited vehemence. It was a triviality, soon forgotten.

But she went around, searching among those she met — searching for the signs of encounters that would say to her: your people.

They came to her through someone now dead, a great poet. In petrified recognition, she read:

> You say: 'Return to your father's hearth,
> To bow for a father's kiss!'
> — your love, to me, is bitter and harsh,
> it strokes and smacks with sticks.
>
> With blows you cleanse, with knives you absolve,
> against your love I brace for a fight,
> it feels like you washed away stains and sores
> along with my star's vigor and light.
>
> With lye you wash my star so clean,
> It makes it clear as water,
> then empties my star of its gleam
> as night in water's mirror.

Your people!

But he was so resolutely determined, so terribly, rashly, blasphemously determined:

'There I wish to sputter alone, far from your despised flame...'

Crisis

That was to join the other side: the side of rebellion.

And yet, what an immense relief it must be to embrace that cause so resolutely, to fall without regret, to seriously and truly fall ... And fall he did, but as a flash of lightning from the Lord...

And then she collapsed in despair at the thought of her own dreams.

Fröding was different. He was clearly ill, whereas she...

Or was she also...?

No, it was something else. It's impossible to imagine looking another, real person in the eye and seeing that they're damned. That kind of thing you can only know about yourself.

Having knowledge of such things means you have no people. You're alone.

And yet not entirely alone. Sometimes even passing close to another person whom you can neither reach nor help can provide a kind of comfort — it's a comfort to think that even disconsolation is collective, that it too can be shared, or at the very least, has led to greater capacity for understanding. There's nothing to be done. There's no point holding out your hand, for the other person isn't likely to perceive the affinity with you anyway. But you can nod to him, as if to your own reflection, and sense that you have someone else to visualize and cling to through the loneliness.

Malin had experienced this once with a little boy in first grade who used to live in Tullinge — an encounter she would never forget.

It was the previous fall. Malin was walking from the train and as she turned up the collar on her winter coat, which had recently proven necessary against the nasty wind and weather, there stood Magnus Anderson in front of her, shivering, and frozen stiff in a tattered sweater, his legs and feet bare. She happened to recognize him from a children's party.

'Please lady,' he said hoarsely, 'Can you spare some change? Pappa is sick and Mamma is so sad. We don't know what to do!'

Malin didn't have any change to give him. The encounter cut through her like a knife.

At home she recounted the story to her mother: *Can't we help them in some way, can you imagine, barefoot in this weather...?*

Her mother appeared more surprised and indignant than compassionate, and it came out that, for one thing, just today Mr. Anderson had passed by, hale and hearty, on his way to the school construction site, where he had presumably been looking for work (which evidently he didn't get, judging from the sullen expression on his face when he returned) — and for another, the Sewing Society had very recently donated socks, shoes and jackets to Magnus and his younger siblings.

This left Malin feeling confused and unsettled. On one side was the apparent deception that filled her with indignation and contempt. On the other was the fact that no parent would send their child out to beg without good reason, so apparently the Andersons still weren't any too flush, even with help from the Sewing Society. But taking away his shoes and socks and sending him out, barefoot in the rain... would of course increase the odds of coming home with something... The crucial point was that Magnus Anderson's feet were as clearly and undeniably bare, his nose just as blue with cold, and the rain as freezing no matter how dishonest or needy his parents were. It was this, the essence of the whole matter, that nothing could be done about. Neither donating more nor advising the Sewing Society to withhold their charity would resolve the matter.

Perhaps the agonizing hopelessness and paralysis of that unsatisfactory conclusion, which was no conclusion at all, had remained undigested in her memory — for it reappeared now, at the sight of Magnus Anderson sitting in his seat. Though he wore socks and shoes and his sweater was no longer tattered, his voice and person remained somehow stunted, timid. The entire weight of everything that could never be remedied or made better, for which no one could even justifiably be held responsible, all of the seemingly meaningless, unavoidable suffering that must be borne and borne, endured and endured

Crisis

— welled over Malin as an indication of the deepest essence of human existence. Lay your hands in your lap, shudder, and watch. Take off your shoes and socks, head out into the rain, hold out your hand and say: 'Please lady...' There was nothing more to it. That was life. She was the only one who sought to avoid it.

That's how it went: what started out as greeting a friend in need inevitably ended the same way: that even a friend would prove to be her judge.

Magnus Anderson sat at his little desk in his first-grade class as Malin's prosecutor: a representative of universal suffering sitting face to face with one who did not want to take suffering upon herself.

Karin Boye

The Forst family, sitting around the dinner table, a completely ordinary dinner table.

Father at the head of the table. As the central figure around which everything else revolves, he would never sit anywhere else. Even seated, his head remains higher than the rest; even silent he emits, commands. It's impossible to say exactly why everyone defers to Father with a respect tinged with fear, even strangers. It's as if even a furious bull or a bolting horse would stop in its tracks at the sound of Father's deep, measured voice of icy will.

Across from him there's Lillan, the darling six-year-old. Malin never ceases to be amazed at the psychological insight a six-year-old can muster in order to wind her way around the shoals and skerries of the family.

Beside Malin on the long side of the table, Mother shrunken in eternal bustle and eternal servitude.

Along the other side of the table, the two brothers finding it hard not to tattle and bicker with each other. Sometimes this elicits a glare from Father. A single glare is always enough.

The Mora grandfather clock ticks loudly, spitefully. It enjoys the privilege of being a blameless object, while dread embraces the living as they are judged. It amuses itself, blatantly, unabashedly while the living sit in silence. The air is charged and tense as always these days.

These days? Was it really just these days? It's conceivable, probable even, that things had always been this charged, since time immemorial. At times it's accepted as inevitable, other times it's insufferable. The boys are probably still young enough to accept fear as part of the air they breathe. The time

Crisis

will come though, when they rise up — whether to be bent or broken or wrest themselves loose.

Certainly, the tension had been there before, and the more she thought about it the surer she became. The strained atmosphere couldn't be attributed to any particular cause, instead, tones of voice dictated its form: when Father spoke it was like coins tossed disdainfully at those who weren't worth anything more — when Mother spoke it was as if she was slipping by in nervous fright, quickly as she could so as not to draw attention to herself. Things never erupted. There were never scenes. Though perhaps not fundamentally a happy one, her parents' marriage nevertheless remained an exemplary one, in which never a harsh word was spoken, for the sake of the children.

Recently the center of tension had shifted from mother to Malin. In that it no longer revolved around Gustav Forst's personal disappointments, but rather a matter of pedagogy, there was no need for him to mince words. However calmly a meal might begin, something inevitably came up before it ended.

But it wasn't just Father who carried an electric charge — or else the atmosphere wouldn't have felt so oppressively stormy. If Father's positive charge filled him with a desire to attack, then Malin was his negatively charged opposite: sitting there, constantly ready to be assailed, her movements timid, her gaze hesitant. Nothing provoked Gustav Forst so wildly — as if he were some horrifying monster!

This double charge generated lightning.

'There's a kid in our class who stole something,' Sölve blurted out of the blue. He couldn't hold his tongue about the day's big event.

'Usch, how sad,' said mother. 'It's terrible when they start so young.'

Sölve's eyes glittered with the sensation of it:

'We had to promise not to mention anyone by name, but he has a very rich dad — a rich pappa, and he gets as much allowance as he likes, but he stole something anyway.'

'Surely he must be ill in some way?' Malin remarked, trembling.

The jolt wasn't in the utterance per se. It was in the wavering of her voice! An all too intimate wavering, as when people speak of their own concern, and moreover, one they hold dear. It was as immodest as a naked body. Anything intimate enough to make your voice waver was not to be mentioned at the dinner table, and not in front of the whole family. And someone who found everything this intimate must remain silent.

He looked up from his plate, his gaze resting on Malin. The tension grew.

'Is that the case? So this is what our future educators are learning at that college. If that's the case then I say, no, thank you very much, we're better off without such schooling. When a poor boy steals he's a thief — but when a rich boy steals then he's sick! If it were up to me I'd call a spade a spade. That boy's a scoundrel and a shame to his family. And to imagine that people could see it any other way!'

'I didn't mean it like that...' stammered Malin.

Her father looked at her for a long time and then said, in a low, deliberate voice that was emphatic with contempt:

'Then why did you say it?'

Even if she had been able to explain everything — if she could take everything from deep inside her and spread it across the table to show she meant something else entirely — that she had no intention of championing the wealthy at the expense of the poor — how could he have forgotten lashing out at her the other day when she defended the fact that non-property owners had a majority in local government — then he had shamed her for standing with the selfish and poor against the selfless and cultured — and now she was supposed be shamed for supporting dishonorable wealthy people at the expense of the poor but honorable...? No matter which way you looked at it, Father was always right. You could be convinced to your core that you were right — but simply hearing the derision in his voice made all self-certainty vanish. No one could ever be in the right but Father.

Crisis

Still, there was much she would have said in her defense — — — had the deluge of tears not overwhelmed her, that perpetual, unwelcome culmination of every situation. No matter how she clenched her fists and resisted, she could never do more than smother the sobbing while the tears streamed, unhindered down her cheeks.

The boys exchanged a knowing glance that said: 'Girls!'

'So, it's this again, what a surprise!' said Father. 'Is it absolutely impossible even to utter a single word, any word, in my own house, without causing these scenes and dramatic outbursts?! Why even bring up such idiotic ideas if you can't tolerate discussing them! *Women!*'

Mother said nothing, but she suffered, and this time she had no choice but to take Father's side. She had long since learned to keep quiet and put up with it — and hadn't cried for a long time. One adapts when one has to. Malin surely ought to have known her father well enough to realize that this modern talk of defending bad behavior would have no effect. It took time to get to the bottom of Father's strict character, she had learned that much from experience, but Malin should have had ample time for that undertaking; she was an adult now.

Is it only the bread that mother is slicing through? Malin watches her mother's movements as if through a haze. Who or what is she actually cutting when she throws all her weight behind that knife? Not a person, no. But something that she dislikes about a person, something that needs to be cut away.

Malin frightens each of her parents without comprehending how. The hostility always about to explode is largely from anxiety, at least in her mother, but Malin remains oblivious to that. She only ever hears the accusation, never the fear underlying it.

After coffee, when the parents are alone, Fru Forst, her eyes downcast, remarks:

'Gustav, don't you think it would be best to take Malin to the doctor?'

'Perhaps,' the man replied.

Karin Boye

She could hear his disapproval in the cold, terse tone of his response. His narrowed, sealed lips conveyed his unspoken disdain: Coddling! Nonsense! Hysterical women!

Perplexed, she sat quietly for a long while, wondering whether to believe his tone or his words, in that they contradicted each other.

'Well, if you don't think it's necessary...' she said diffidently at last, as if in retreat.

But something resembling pity had stirred in his grey eyes. He threw his wife a kindly glance as if she were a poor little animal at his feet — a timid, but in its own way touching, little animal without a will of its own. It was an uplifting and supportive gaze. Whatever his faults, his strength of spirit was more than enough for the both of them. She looked up at him in gratitude: she had waited so long to see that expression on his face! Oh, Gustav!

'You should be a bit more convinced of what *you* yourself think, at the very least. As far as *I* am concerned you're more than welcome to try taking her to the doctor,' he answered.

'Malin asked to go, too.'

'Ahhh! —All the more reason! Well, I'd be very surprised if a doctor could do anything about the matter. It's a question of upbringing, not of medication.'

'But you do still think that we could at least try?'

'By all means. Just go.'

After this brief loving moment, he turned away in disdain from his wife and the whole of her sex that allowed itself be so cowed.

Crisis

But which doctor to choose? — It would have to be one with sensible views about life who approached matters calmly. One of Fru Forst's good friends had recommended a Doctor Ringström in Lärkstaden: he was wise and had a good sense of humor about everything. Once, when the friend had accidentally swallowed a crown from her tooth and in her dismay called Doctor Ringström (who admittedly was a nerve specialist, but still a doctor and the husband of her good friend), he answered simply: 'What a pity, Elsa, crowns are so expensive these days.' — That made her laugh; she was reassured.

Elsa was not the only one who spoke highly of Doctor Ringström. Similar opinions were voiced in many circles: he was level-headed; a realist with a good head on his shoulders; someone who had seen much and knew more; all told, a man of worldly wisdom.

All of this had made a good impression on Fru Forst. Most important in a case like Malin's would be to find a sensible man. So she called him, and they decided Malin would go in on Sunday. She finished too late at the teacher's college to go in the evening and ought not to miss any work.

On Sunday morning she stood at the window, looking out at the hill where the sun glistened upon the snow. Sunny or cloudy, snowy or green, it made no difference. It lay far away, as if in another time. Two days before, a tree had blown over and its branches had whipped against the window. Malin had sat there without really noticing it.

'What was that?' her mother had called out, rushing in from the next room.

'A tree blew over, I think,' Malin replied without turning around.

'And you're supposed to be the nervous one!' her mother sighed. It took more than trees blowing over to reach Malin. That all happened out there, outside the wall. Inside the wall everything was only: anguish. It seeped in, filling every void, formless, without content. It was everything. So here she stood, watching as the sun shone on the snow out there in the external world she could not reach, thinking: Will this truly change anything? And if so, what? Can they help me? Can they break through the wall?

She was hardly a person any longer. She existed as a kind of bundle that could be placed and positioned anywhere, but which couldn't move on its own.

'Can't you just go on your own?' mother asked. 'It hardly seems necessary for me to go with you. I'll barely make it back again in time to make the soup, and you're the one that he'll be talking to anyway, I know nothing about it. Put on your coat and go on your own!'

Slowly, slowly Malin walked toward the door to obey but sank down into a chair in the hallway. Cry, would she have to cry again, yes, she couldn't make it on her own. She didn't care about feeling ashamed anymore, her pride was gone. Forces stronger than she might as well take hold of her; she no longer had the strength to resist.

Mother pulled her up from the chair. Malin slowly followed her mother's example and put on her coat.

The ground outside had already been thawing and then freezing; today it had begun to thaw again, leaving the streets slick and icy. Malin doesn't understand how she'll dare walk on them. She realizes that's foolish — mother has already set forth — but she can't muster the immense energy required to risk it. Falling trees might not rattle her, a brick to the head would almost be amusing — just a question of accepting and enduring. But to act! To dare! To exert her will!

So it's mother's will instead and even though Malin doesn't dare, neither does she have the strength to counter another,

Crisis

stronger will. In a struggle between two kinds of weakness the worst one wins out — so, terrified and in agony, she proceeds.

No, you think: you'll never make the train. And after you've climbed aboard, you think: it'll never depart. It doesn't matter which trees and bushes and houses fly past, they're probably the same old ones, no reason to perceive them any differently — only the strange thing is that time is also flying. And yet time never, ever passes, instead, more time arrives bearing the same anguish, it's never ending, it's inexhaustible. Why does it have to be so inexhaustible? Why couldn't enough be enough, just one time?

At last, they found themselves sitting in Doctor Ringström's vacant waiting room on a Sunday.

If one were to take the trouble of finding out about Doctor Ringström's life history, one would see that his reputation for pragmatism seemed to be well-founded. Even his schoolmates would confirm that it wasn't for lack of intelligence that Sixten Ringström's light hadn't shone particularly brightly in school. It was more that he lacked ambition. Perhaps even then he had viewed the overbearing eagerness to increase knowledge with an instinctive, skeptical derision. Perhaps even then he sensed how disappointingly fast one got to the bottom of things. — After graduating he took advantage of all the opportunities that went along with being a rich man's son and spent long periods abroad. He had seen large parts of the world at an age when most people had barely seen beyond the town where they were born. His anecdotes and intimations confirmed that he truly had experienced a great deal, that much was evident to those who knew him, but he never related anything more substantial, whether because by this point he had left his experiences as a young man so far behind that he no longer derived any pleasure from recalling them, or because, despite being so young, he already had something of the wisdom of Ecclesiastes in his blood; he was born disappointed. — Moreover, it was while traveling that he came to choose his career in medicine. Certain manifestations of malaria in the tropics piqued his interest, as strange as that may sound. In effect, it was pure ennui that prompted him to enter the field of medicine — detective novels had ultimately proved too simple for his relatively well-equipped mind — and to his surprise he discovered that he not only possessed a general aptitude for science, but also, more astonishingly, he experienced a sudden burst of interest in it. Admittedly this dissipated during medical school, but by that time it had served its purpose, driving him onto one of the all too many paths that had stood open to him, and his suddenly-flowering interest disappeared without his missing it. He chose a specialization in nerves, however, because of its marketability.

Stories circulated from his university days when his vacation destinations of choice were continental cities, and society ladies whispered piquantly that he had led something of an adventurous life. That he always held himself to the standards of a young man of his position and never took unnecessary risks was best demonstrated by the fact that his adventures never hindered his career in any way.

Upon passing his exams, which he did easily and in fact with very high marks, he was dealt a tough blow: it came out that his father, that rich man, was actually teetering on the verge of financial ruin. As Sixten Ringström would jokingly say to his intimate friends, he occasionally looked in the mirror in the morning to see whether his hair had turned white overnight — that's how bad it had been at the time. He found himself facing the realities of life as he never had before. Although everything eventually sorted itself out with the help of intervening relatives and his marriage to a rich, pretty heiress, he nonetheless emerged from these trials somewhat changed — it left him 'deepened,' as his family put it. Since then, the practice that he founded had blossomed unusually fast, not simply because both his family and his wife had extensive and influential circles of acquaintances, but equally, and perhaps more so, because his personality radiated a cultured sophistication and natural charm that quickly made him a doctor *en vogue*.

Considering Doctor Ringström's varied life history, it was hardly surprising that people spoke of his worldly wisdom.

Crisis

Some might say that, effectively, there was nothing left for him to be curious about anymore (notwithstanding that most 'private question' as he once told a close friend, 'When does my cherished father-in-law actually intend to relinquish his worldly existence?'). He often related Albert Engström's story about an old man who was warned against drinking wood alcohol: 'You'll go blind!' — he was told, to which he replied: 'So be it, I've pretty much seen it all!' One female patient even called the knowing smile of disillusionment that subsequently flashed across Doctor Ringström's face demonic.

To paint a complete portrait of the man, however, one would in all fairness have to include witnesses holding an opinion that diverged significantly from general consensus.

Truth be told there were perhaps only two people who found him naïve. He had no idea, and even if he had, he wouldn't have taken their opinions seriously. The word naïve didn't even exist in the vocabulary of these two people, but even so, they were well versed in this nameless quality, and it provoked their scorn. The people in question were Doctor Ringström's two oldest children, ages seven and five.

Jan, the five-year-old, had looked away when his father explained that his new baby brother had been purchased at the NK department store. It was obvious from his father's voice that this explanation defied all reason. He could hear it, even if adults seemed to have difficulty distinguishing such things. And anyway, that was too simple an explanation. There had to be some *big* explanation, that much was apparent in the fact that his father had gone to the trouble of lying in the first place. Some big, maybe even terrible explanation. Maybe one that was terrible and funny at the same time. It was just hard to know where to find the right source of information. Since it was clear that their father needed them to believe him, and it was decidedly less complicated to go along with the ideas that grown-ups came up with, that's what he did, though to be on the safe side, he still avoided looking him in the eyes.

Maj-Britt, on the other hand, met her father's look with ingenuous openness. The risk of being seen through was minuscule, that much she knew from experience. She could

Karin Boye

think whatever she wanted. She had already seen Mamma feed the baby and her instincts groped nervously and formlessly around the underlying secret like the shadows of sea creatures and algae undulating in the dark depths far below. The children tried to reconcile the appearance of their baby brother with all kinds of contexts, one after the other, and with functions and mysteries of their own bodies, but NK — that they resolutely refused to accept. And to think he actually believed she had swallowed that!

After their father left, they sat quietly a moment. Although the siblings didn't quite trust each other enough to exchange impressions, and they wouldn't have found the right words anyway, they each stood, cold and superior, possessing a clarity that would have translated into adult speech as: Doctor Ringström is woefully naïve.

It was not the first time they had ascertained that fact, nor would it be the last. A minor incident had occurred just that morning. Jan had refused to drink his gruel because his cup was the kind of cup that made nasty faces at you when you drank out of it. *That* part remained unmentioned, of course, but as he searched for some other excuse, Mamma betrayed his secret (it's not that she was unintelligent, she was just insensitive. Guard your deepest self at all costs, for in vulnerable moments others crudely exploit any weakness exposed in childlike confidence.) Pappa just shrugged his shoulders and said, 'What a poetic excuse — but if the boy's full, then let him be excused.' — Leaving the table, Jan's gratitude blended with the pity of the craftier party: fortunately, Doctor Ringström remained oblivious for the most part.

The doctor chuckled to himself as he stepped down to his office to receive his patient. Cups that make faces! The little scoundrel sure was imaginative! He made a secret wish for the boy never to fall in with those most amusing liars, the poets! (His aversion was not in any way related to their capacity to be either amusing or liars, but rather to their low standard of living.)

Crisis

The two ladies entered, and Doctor Ringström politely stood up from his seat behind the desk. He made a pleasingly gentlemanlike impression.

'I understand you are Fru Forst. And then this must be the little patient?'

He instantly recognized the figure standing before him: an intellectually inclined young girl, erotically unawakened, and studious to the point of overexertion. A pocket-sized, female Hamlet, presumably. According to what Fru Forst had said on the phone there were no particularly difficult complications. There were no actual psychotic symptoms.

Malin shook his outstretched hand, scrutinizing his face at the same time. Sure, he looked handsome and friendly, but distant, just as most people remain far away when they aren't themselves seeking help. That's the way it was: she sought his help and therefore drew near him, but he had no need of hers and was consequently far away from her. But she too could have contributed assistance, by virtue of being another case — she could help solve a medical problem. She was at his disposal, and at the disposal of science, as a crossword puzzle ready to be solved. Of course she had no idea what he would ask her, yet remained adamantly determined to answer clearly, exactly, sincerely all the same. — But when it came down to it, she probably wouldn't be a very interesting case to him. He likely treated countless young people who had difficulty sleeping and who cried too easily. He surely understood that sort of thing inside out. No, she couldn't claim to be especially interesting to him, that much she understood. But still, maybe a little! As least as interesting as the others?

'And how old are you, Fröken Forst?' Doctor Ringström asked in his pleasant voice as he wrote in his journal.

'Twenty. And five months.'

'Right then. Twenty. And you're not sleeping at night?'

'Just a little. A few hours.'

'A few hours? How many is that?'

'Two — three — four — five.'

'That's not enough, when you're so young.'

Karin Boye

He glanced up with a winning smile. He had such beautiful teeth.

'I take it you lie awake worrying? About the world's mysteries?'

Malin searched for a precise answer. Was she contemplating the world's mysteries? Hardly. Her difficulties were purely personal and had more to do with her will than her thoughts.

But before she could answer, Doctor Ringström smiled again and continued:

'You know what, I'll let you in on a secret: worrying won't help a bit. We have to be content knowing that the mysteries of existence will never be solved. That is if they aren't figments of our imagination in the first place.'

Malin awaited further questions.

Only twenty years old! thought Doctor Ringström. And there she sits, looking so tragic, as if anyone her age could know anything about problems. Only an optimist still wet behind the ears would bother running to the doctor complaining of that well-known, existential pain that everyone normally goes through in their twenties. This one has yet to see real sorrow. She knows nothing of real life. Of course, she should get married; all young girls should. But then, you can't say that to this kind of twenty-year-old, who can't take the least hint of cynicism, and would get upset. It's fortunate for the medical profession that nature created that aspect of life to be less pressing for women than for men.

'Presumably you don't have any serious problems to speak of?' he said suddenly, 'I mean, financial problems, for instance?'

'No.'

'No, we've always spared the children anything like that,' Fru Forst confirmed.

'Wisely done! An excellent principle by which to raise children!' said the doctor.

'You see, Fröken Forst, these are the truly serious concerns in life. Until you've experienced them you can't understand what real sorrow is. The mysteries of existence look like child's play in comparison.

Crisis

And something else I hope you'll take to heart, your health is more important than your grades — and more important to your future as well, though it might not seem like it now.'

Yet another faint smile spread inadvertently across his face. How could she possibly sit there looking so tragic with a nose like that? he thought. No style to her. Niobe with a snub nose. A twenty-year old Niobe with a snub nose!

Out loud, he said:

'You know, Fröken Forst, I can't imagine anything in the world serious enough to justify the look on your face right now. Neither money nor grades.'

He waited for a laugh there, and it vexed him that she didn't crack a smile. The girl was completely devoid of humor; that was apparent. Stiffening somewhat, he took a blood test and confirmed she was anemic, which was not an insignificant factor. Mystery solved.

Silently, he scribbled a prescription for an arsenic and valerian solution. Handing it to Fru Forst, he treated them to the same, sympathetic, gentlemanly bow and then smiled again, as if nothing at all disturbing had happened.

'So, no more contemplating the world's mysteries! And keep this in mind as well: grades can always come second!' he repeated, turning toward Malin.

With that, Malin understood that the consultation was over, and she burst into tears.

That was really all there would be.

'Well now, promise to take your medicine as the doctor ordered,' said Mother once they were back on the train. 'That certainly was an expensive visit!'

'Yes,' Malin replied.

She sat rigidly, staring straight ahead. It's not much consolation, when all of one's hopes for continued existence rest on an admittedly large bottle of arsenic and valerian. It's not much, but at least it's something.

Karin Boye

She had a peculiar dream.

She was walking through an autumn forest of tall, shiny, sonorous tree trunks like metal pipes, dead leaves around her feet, the end of everything, walking and walking, aimlessly, just to get away, and she got farther and farther away, to where she would never meet anyone again, yet couldn't get away from what she wished to escape, because she carried that inside her, a despairing anguish that sought to blow her apart, she could give it no expression, had to yowl like a dog, as loudly as she could, howling uncontrollably. For no clear reason, she had to. Nobody heard her, nobody would ever hear her, she would walk forever through this dead forest and howl forever. Somehow, she could never howl enough and the thought occurred to her: this is what it is to be mentally ill, it's here, just as I expected it... Now I know how it is. This is the end, it's over. From this point on it will continue forever.

Crisis

Morning prayer is one of the seven circles of hell. It provides powerful support for torturing and tormenting one's conscience, while not being powerful enough to vanquish such selfish defiance. To be torn is torture. And so exhaustingly grueling that you're left faint and soaked with sweat as if having made some great effort while under an enormous strain though not even fifteen minutes of the working day has passed. You resist, you try to think about other things, but you have no strength to hold your ground, so you submit and sink deeper and still deeper into the abyss of bad conscience.

Principal Melling steps up to the lectern with a brisk determination. Though she nearly disappears behind it she's somehow never the least bit ridiculous. (As long as it is cold out, morning prayers are held in the ugly, brown music room — it costs too much to heat the large assembly hall just for the morning.) Principal Melling is severe with herself. Usually born of her own self-examination, her morning prayers come from the heart, her words delivered in a harsh and unsentimental tone that causes Malin pain. If only it was a matter of enduring pain! Instead, in some secluded recess of her soul, resistance is provoked into being, as if responding to some flagrant injustice. And that contradiction, in turn, incites her conscience to clamp down all the more viciously... Malin yearns to run, to flee with her open wounds out of the rain of salt, but with so much of her normal self-control intact she stays where she is, despite everything. She squirms, she clenches and unclenches her fists, she sighs inaudibly to herself, she grits her teeth, she tries to harden herself — and she remains where she is. The valerian helps some, too; like a

Karin Boye

thin film over the surface, it helps her avoid committing any worse foolishness.

Principal Melling's discussion today is about the right kind of contrition.

... how pitiful, how hollow we can be ourselves in our contrition...

MALIN 1. That's true, like the terrible presentation I gave in fifth grade on Norwegian cities and industry. I was ashamed and was filled with regret about it, but in a pitiful and vain way. To this day I still feel myself blushing deeply with pitiful, vain regret. I'm rotten to the core with pitifulness, and all my pitiful soul's interest is focused on my own pitiful little person...

MALIN 2. Maybe that's not really important?

MALIN 1. It's not important in the least, as long as it doesn't cause you to imagine you're even fit to tie another's shoe. It wouldn't be important in the least but for the fact that your vanity is so frenzied that you then bemoan your own pitifulness — and even that is done pitifully and so vainly that sorrow itself becomes pitiful, and regret, too, becomes pitiful itself, pitiful to the innermost core.

... while on the other hand, we treat something that actually is worthy of regret as a mere mishap, as something we're only too glad to dismiss...

MALIN 2. But wouldn't we be better off if we did just dismiss it?

MALIN 1. Better off? Don't we do that already? Don't we try to imagine any other alternative than the one, real solution, namely submission? Going around and around postponing what will inevitably come to be, imagining that salvation is possible without being willing to do absolutely *anything*. Believing that God can be — conciliatory. It's so pitiful of me to try to make God pitiful too.

... but such errors — even ones that seem inconsequential at first glance — might very well be taken as warning signals — clear signs that our relationship to God lacks depth and tenacity...

MALIN 1. Lacks depth and tenacity! Fortunate, fortunate are those who have not slid further down that slope! Those who can still talk about having a relationship with God! Those who haven't yet strayed so far as to be in complete and utter darkness!

MALIN 2. Let me out of here! I can't bear listening anymore! The anguish is suffocating! Every word, every judgmental inflection. I don't want to be judged! I want out!

MALIN 1. You're just a cowardly wretch who doesn't dare look the truth in the eye! You will stay, you will see, you will listen and understand what you really are... And you'll be judged. That is only right and just. Barely enough to be called right and just!

... but contrition that aligns with God's heart is the only thing that can bring about a true change of heart, a deepening of our spiritual lives...

MALIN 1. I agree. And that's why all of my anguish, all of my despair is inconsequential, just smoke in the wind, a sin to be borne — that is, if we can imagine eternity in its full measure.

MALIN 2. I wish I could at least throw a fit, weep, break free!

MALIN 1. Just stay put and hear this out. You will see yourself, in all of your wretchedness, you will endure still more of it, it will do you such good — I hate you.

... Our Father, who art in Heaven ...

MALIN 1. '... and justly deserve Thy eternal punishment ...'

Karin Boye

As she raised her head from her prayers, her gaze came to rest on the nape of Siv Lindvall's neck. A lovely, slim pillar extending like a gentle hymn from perfectly sloping shoulders. The most wonderful thing happened; Malin's tense, tormented muscles eased for an instant, she relaxed, her restlessly wandering eyes found a focus, the judgment of her thoughts dissolved into the exquisite, liberating play of lines before her. Containing her thoughts usually required so much exertion, but this was effortless. Her thoughts remained steady and unwavering; she couldn't tear herself away.

A liberation. A miracle.

When the psalm had ended, the rows of benches emptied, one after the other, and Malin was swept up, dazed, into the stream. She walked out, engrossed in wonder. Her experience of deliverance had been enigmatic. Not forever, not protracted, but just long enough to allow an unhappy creature to catch her breath.

Perhaps everything exquisite has some mystical repose to grant. Miraculous and holy.

She had experienced something like this before, though. Sometimes, feeling tired and dejected, she deliberately walked a different way home from school and passed a house that was beautiful in its pure, balanced proportions. Soaking up the form of the building, or rather letting herself be soaked up by it, relieved her exhaustion somewhat. During the time of anguish, it was as if the outside world had withdrawn completely and left her alone with her merciless inner struggle. Now it seemed as if the outside world had granted her a moment of mercy and incomprehensible consolation.

Underneath her resigned gratitude a tiny, feverish hope stirred: dare she count on it happening again?

Karin Boye

Malin was to travel to Uppsala for the final days of Easter vacation to visit Nora Hermansson who was studying there. They had met a few times at summer meetings of the High School Christian League and Nora had often been a kind of mother confessor to Malin, though since Nora had begun her studies they seldom saw each other. Deep down Malin didn't want to go. Of course, the thought of a few days' reprieve from the dinner table outbursts at home was tempting, but so many other embarrassments would surely take their place. Malin neither expected anyone to help, nor hoped for any relief from her current circumstances. Nora was among those whose respect Malin very much wished to earn — but simply preserving what little sympathy Nora might have for her, would, in her current state, cause Malin such exertion that she doubted she could even manage that. In some ways, it was a trip to the bitter destination of losing a friend. But Mother had been so optimistic about this little change of scenery. And it's not as if Malin, given the state she was in, felt that she deserved anyone's respect anyway.

The first day had been insufferable. Malin tried to keep her chin up and act as if nothing were the matter, but that resulted in such tension that the conversation stalled. In the evening, when they sat up in Nora's little attic room, drinking steaming cups of tea under the cozy light of a lamp, Malin asked, in the clearest language and most concrete, staccato tone that she could muster whether psychology wasn't an incredibly important subject that ought to be introduced much earlier in school, and above all, continue to be studied at a more mature age as well, especially since there was so

Crisis

much that was still unknown and surprising, and so much more to it that no one really knew what to do with? Something or other in their conversation made Nora pull a book down from the bookshelf to read a diary entry by a famous English psychologist where he referred to 'The Human Bible,' by which he meant the human soul, and not even its more beautiful aspects, but rather its mysterious, unknown, 'amazing, if not always amusing' aspects. That's what he called *the human Bible*... In the face of such all-encompassing compassion Malin lost her equilibrium entirely and burst into a deluge of tears.

She raged against herself, but that accomplished nothing. Was crying really the only language she had left? Unknown immensities seethed within her, she ascended Alpine peaks and plunged into deep abysses, dreaded nightmarish terrors and had only miracles to hope for — outwardly, however, it was only ever expressed in one form: tears, tears, tears. As monotonous and incomprehensible as the tentative sounds made by a deaf-mute... Her tears fell, not soothingly as with rain or dew, but violently, spurting forth with the overwhelming pressure of a geyser, a torrent of heat, hurling itself in vain up into a merciful sky, all too distant. A language no one could decipher. She did actually have a sea of questions to ask, scores of experiences to relate — but could only ever convey them in this single, incomprehensible way. And what kind of questions were these really? None that could be clearly formulated. And what kind of experiences? None that could be told to others. They dwelt, instead, on the other side of words, beyond the ineffable, and she could do nothing but wait, wait until she might reemerge to exist in the world where words convey meaning between humans — or, alternatively, plunge even deeper into the place where the words we do have designate nothing and reach the place where humans remain inaccessible to one another.

Nora accepted the outburst calmly, not letting it affect her and pretending, at least, to see it as a completely natural form of agreement. Malin was overwhelmed with gratitude. It was as if her worth as a normal human being had not been entirely destroyed.

Karin Boye

The evening concluded with the peace and tranquility that invariably followed one of Malin's tearful outbursts, those moments she needn't feel ashamed.

But the following morning, when Nora had to leave early for a lecture, something else happened. Sitting in the corner of the sofa, looking around the room, a feeling of doubt verging on horror came over Malin. The chairs in their floral chintz covers, the sofa with its crocheted antimacassar, the shelf of teacups, the smooth white tiled stove, all seemed to reveal their nature as incidental and specious veneers, a surface of material things she had relinquished long ago. She felt now as if she were moving through a place where forms had been vanquished, as if she were spreading herself, formlessly, in ur-matter itself, like a dead person slowly sinking back through worlds of dissolution, in a race backwards through creation, drawing ever nearer to the regenerating ur-nebulae, the hearth of the Mothers.

She was gripped by a fit of shaking in the face of something so simple as to be unknowable — perhaps the very fact of existence lay revealed before her — holy — holy — holy — —

Nora returned home to find her guest in a state of disintegration. She listened attentively to her befuddled attempts at explanation ('material itself is holy — drawing the shoes off of your feet — denuded of body and soul — much too holy for me —'), to then deliver a succinct and precise diagnosis: 'You are definitely unwell! You're ill!' — upon which she put Malin to bed.

'I have to go out for a while now,' she said later that afternoon, 'but find a book to read, something with a *plot line*, all right? Don't sit here thinking about the stove and matter and all that. Now promise to be good and do as I say. I'll be back in twenty minutes or so.'

Malin produced a little smile. No, she wouldn't think any more today. She could feel that the worst had passed for now and she could catch her breath for a bit.

Obediently, she took Kipling down from the bookshelf and sat in the window. Outside the trees stood naked against an overcast sky, and for some reason, they were closer to her than they had been for a long time. They stood as if life had colored them faintly, which could only mean that a new, weak drop of life had fallen into her own eye — as if there were still an adventure to be had somewhere, perhaps even a little longing to get out — — —

Yes, it was longing she felt. A longing that pulsed with life, not with the usual, dead anxiety she was accustomed to. A longing that was in search of something, rather than spinning around tediously. She felt something approximating the feeble, tentative sprouting of a will.

Where do I want to be? Where do I belong? she gingerly tested her longing. The response engulfed her from deep below, like a flame, rising to fill her tiniest recesses:

I want to see Siv. I want to be where Siv is.

What was that!? Wasn't that — — —

She clamped her mouth shut, defending herself from the words. Words lead you astray; she didn't want to know them. She stood there motionless in silent expectation, and even the terror that grazed her for an instant was still and solemn.

The day after tomorrow she would be at the teachers' college again. That would clarify everything.

Blessed be longing that is alive! Blessed be life that is alive!

Karin Boye

She returned to find everyone busy chatting and catching up after the Easter break. Siv was standing beside a shelf of books, speaking with Peggy, with whom she shared a desk.

And so it was true.

It was true from her innermost organ out to her skin, out to the smallest pinpoint on her skin, it was a kind of instantaneous vitalization, the intense feeling of being naked through her clothes, it was fire; its suddenness was almost painful. Yet she made no drastic movement, didn't cry out, didn't even take a step, she just stood, unmoving, ablaze. Her eyes, however, darted about, starving for detail after tiny detail of the only real face — clinging to it, drowning in it. Home! She expanded in a deep breath of relief. There was no line, no curve, no variation that did not yield the same, longed-for answer. Home, home at last! And as she stood there, submitting herself unconditionally to the delicate yet steely rhythms, they enveloped her in their restoring coolness. It was as if their grandeur and strength flowed over her as well and she drank and drank of their golden, abundant calm.

It lasted for one motionless moment; no one around her noticed.

You, lips, I implore you to clamp so hard upon the unsayable, that not a word slips out to assert its malicious pettiness and obfuscation! Be still, thoughts, don't interrupt, for you have no idea what this is! This only happens once in your life, and never again. Don't give it a name, let it be just as it is, here in my blood and my eyes, life and sap! The wonder of new creation need not be named.

Crisis

That joyous, unnamed intoxication might last for one day — two days, three.

But then your thoughts begin to laugh beneath your pillow as you sleep. You defend yourself in vain, you cowardly insect!

Something that happens once and never again! It has happened thousands upon thousands of times and will happen thousands upon thousands more! Do you not know what it is?

And the insect writhes and groans, sits up, forced to admit: Yes, I do!

Well — and then?

Yes, then. The end.

Karin Boye

A sleepless night was followed by an examination day. Topic: Christianity. Students in classes IV, A and B had each chosen one prophet for a specialized study and were now being evaluated on their work. They were sitting in different classrooms where the desks could be moved far apart from each another. With a timid, oh so timid, forbidden glance, Malin confirmed that Siv had been given a seat behind her and she wouldn't be able to see her during the exam. It was just as well — as it was going to end anyway! At that moment, she felt with smarting clarity just how much she had come to depend on the splendid and mystical solace that only that ivory neck and two perfectly sloping shoulders could grant her... In their regular classroom, Siv sat a bit in front of her, allowing Malin to glance in her direction whenever she liked. At each peek, a pleasant coolness rippled through her entire, tortured ego, easing knots of anxiety and nausea. Admittedly it was only for a brief moment, but it was enough, more than enough even. It was an extravagant abundance. It was life's inherent, precious value.

And yet it would, and indeed must, end.

Malin's forehead bowed even more deeply over her paper. There was no longer anything in front of her to long for. It had to be that way. With her heart's anguish disconnected in some mechanical way from the task at hand, she attempted to write her answers without thinking, as if lifting an overwhelming yet unavoidable burden: '2) The image of God changes: the god of a finite tribe expands into the God of all the world...'

Jeremiah! He had possessed the strength to endure anything for the sake of that inexorably burning voice he heard within him. But she... There was no holy, burning voice within her. All that burned within her was a thirst for the forbidden after a single look cast in that direction.

The tears began to well up again, quietly, almost imperceptibly. She hadn't cried for several days now... The road began sloping downward again, toward disintegration — of course she recognized this, but there was no other to take. Nothing ahead of her, only farther and farther down into the anguish. As her conscience commanded. The dream of the autumn forest! Would she reach it soon? Her hand gripped her pen but she couldn't write any more. Sinking into the morass, sinking into the morass...

The clock continued to tick, time passed, and she had to write, but she didn't.

Jeremiah, Jeremiah, *Jeremiah!* Was there nothing that could spur her interest in Jeremiah, for even an hour? Nothing that could jolt her out of this deathly paralysis just long enough to complete the exam?

All that came to mind were some verses that would be absolutely unsuitable to write about. They were passages she had read so many times that she knew them by heart. The chapter when the prophet, after being imprisoned and exiled, reassures the complaining Baruk: 'The Lord saith thus: Behold, that which I have built will I break down, and that which I have planted I will pluck up, even this whole land. And seekest thou great things for thyself? Seek them not: for, behold, I will bring evil upon all flesh, saith the Lord: but thy life will I give unto thee for a prize in all places whither thou goest.'

Small consolation that is. Then again, that's what made it so magnificent. First the admonishment: 'You're desiring things for which you're unworthy! Control your desires!' — there was a wonderful, merciless justice to this, a far cry from the mercy she prayed for in such a cowardly way. And then cruelty: 'Thy life will I give unto thee as a prize!' — life, bare, unadorned life lay at the heart of all misery of the flesh — like spoils seized — such was God's own annihilating irony, no one else could be so splendidly cruel. Naked life, stripped of all honor, stripped of all joy, stripped of any proximity to what it loves — life as prize — *more than you deserve...*

Even life itself is more than you deserve!

And yet. Perhaps Jeremiah and Baruk held life in higher regard than we do today. Perhaps in their day *life* meant more than just daily digestion and blood circulating. — What she wouldn't give for *life* — she who was on the way toward living death — — —

Something knotted decisively inside her. Suddenly, she realized that everything else was insignificant. She yearned to win her life, *her own life*, and nothing else — as a prize.

Crisis

Last night God succumbed.

Perhaps it was just the hollow shell of a name that went under.

But that shell of a name drew with it the powers of death. I cast it off.

I see objects as they are, unwitting of the names attributed to them. I cast off their names.

I stand, utterly new, on the shore of a sea. Conscience is no longer mine. I cast it off.

The will to life has made me naked. The will to life has made me see. I shall meet whatever comes with naked, open eyes.

Dialogue II: On The Meaning of Pious Words

PRIOR. My son, it has come to my attention recently that you have begun entertaining thoughts of a suspect nature. Is that true? Are you troubled by doubt?

MONK. Not in the least! Either some deceiver is trying to slander me, or — more likely — there has been some mistake. Doubt is the last word I would use to describe the trivial speculations that occur to me during the hours we devote to gardening and woodwork, in accordance with the rules of the order. In fact, they are more akin to pious reflections, for they are of an entirely edifying nature. I am both dismayed and astounded that the rumor mill has deemed this worthy of notice and dismayed above all that the matter has reached your ears in such a distorted state. In that I am thoroughly confident of their innocent nature, I gladly and gratefully submit my reflections to your righteous examination, my venerable Father.

PRIOR. Let us not forget that the tempter is even capable, on occasion, of assuming the form of an innocent child. Be that as it may, I have never doubted either your obedience or your good will, my son.

MONK. May I prove myself worthy of your confidence. — What have they said?

PRIOR. It has been said that you deny the Holy Scriptures.

MONK. If that is so, then I have been grossly misunderstood. But I can also see how such a distortion might have come about. Will you allow me to explain the situation from beginning to end, though it might take me a while to reach my conclusion?

PRIOR. Speak, my son! That is why I am here.

Karin Boye

MONK. Let me first ask, my venerable Father: do you believe that a blind person would understand if you or some other sighted person tried to describe the brilliant colors of an admirable altarpiece?

PRIOR. Speaking as a human, that seems improbable.

MONK. Improbable, or rather... impossible.

Let me ask another question: if a man, with his sense of sight intact, who has held a cane in his hands many times, but who has been deaf from birth — could suddenly hear as the rest of us do — do you believe that this man would understand what the word *cane* meant if he heard the word pronounced?

PRIOR. No, I do not believe so. Though I submit this caveat: we are discussing mortal knowledge, but a higher wisdom exists. For God, nothing is impossible.

MONK. Naturally, always with that caveat, venerable Father!

One must point to the cane while at the same time saying: 'Cane!' to the man who has newly regained his hearing.

On the other hand, people who both see and hear can talk to each other about a cane without any significant difficulty, because we have heard the word uttered so many times, at the same time that we have seen the thing itself. Likewise, if I wished for children to understand what a horse was, children who had never seen a horse before, then I would take them to a horse, point, and say: 'See, that is a horse!' I can also choose simply to explain what a horse is — and my disciple would understand me in that I have so many comparisons and similarities of which to avail myself: a horse is as tall as my shoulders, brown as my habit, and is a living creature. It has four legs like a dog, and the hair in its tail is coarse, coarser than the hair we have on our heads — and many other such statements.

PRIOR. This all seems true and accurate, and I see now why you are such an esteemed teacher at the monastery school.

MONK. Oh, I would not presume to think so. But if I may, I will continue.

When I had reached this point, I thought: if this is how things are in the world of external things — how are they in the world within us? How is a teacher to instruct children or even older students, for that matter, about piety, love, beatitude, or spirit before they have ever seen piety, love, beatitude, or spirit? We can draw a comparison, not with the blind — for surely God could not have created us blind to our inner life — nor with the deaf man who could suddenly hear, for they are more like the poorly instructed child, who hears these words without understanding what they refer to. What, then, do they then imagine when they hear these words?

PRIOR. Well, well, this might cast your ability to teach students in a different light. Anytime you wish you can show school children what you mean by using stories that illustrate the conduct and words of holy men and women.

MONK. I am speaking of our inner life, that from which outer life issues forth. Deeds and words may be the fruits of a pious state of mind, but they might also be an empty illusion. We can never point to a deed and say: this is piety — this is love. One who has already felt true piety, true love, or seen it streaming directly from a pious and loving person, he will understand, he will be able to recognize the same beautiful things in the stories of the saints. But let us imagine someone who has never encountered true piety either in himself or in others, and has only pursued external illusion. Then when his teacher — he too, a man of illusion — lets him read a legend about piety and then explains: 'See, that is piety!' — how can he not comprehend the saint's interior life as being akin to the thoughts and concerns of his instructor? And even if, in spite of everything, a spark of that true piety persisted in the words of the legend and shone through — would he not still run the risk of confusing that dimly glittering spark with the gorgeous, but inauthentic illusion radiating from his teacher? — Or consider one who has never felt true love for Our Savior or his Mother or seen it with his own eyes — if he is taught by a teacher who is equally inexperienced, who feels only the fear of sin all the while referring to this fear as 'love of God' — how can he not then adopt the designations of his teacher, so that he too then imagines 'love of God' to be more a fear of sin than anything else? — And thus it follows that the beautiful

Karin Boye

name of one single, internal quality can conceal ten thousand different realities, including ones that contradict the original intention so profoundly that they might be considered the worst adversaries of the original!

Here, at last, I have arrived at what has been so nefariously distorted. I mean, namely, that not even the holiest of scriptures can avoid this fate of being misunderstood according to the nature and experiences of those reading them. Regardless of all the exegesis and explication by church fathers, and the thousands of commentaries ratified by synod after synod, the bare words remain a puzzle the solution to which is held exclusively by those who have actually encountered, in life and spirit, what the words convey.

PRIOR. I am beginning to understand you. And I am beginning at the same time to understand that no nefarious distortion has in fact taken place. This path you have embarked upon, my son, is a dangerous one. Following it would shake the foundations of our faith.

MONK. Far from it, Father! When I say that words alone teach us nothing about what is innermost and highest, what I actually mean is that it's the living spirit, imbued in human form, that can teach us everything! When such a person stands facing another, someone who has yet to experience an act of spirit — that person will perceive it immediately and comprehend. One smile, one gesture of the hand while walking amid the multitudes will teach any and all who see it to understand what it is to love fearlessly — and better than any book in the world could. Spirit ignites spirit, adding link upon link, creating a holy chain through the ages, never broken, unending. This is the true Apostolic succession that began in the days of our Lord Jesus Christ (and please, venerable Father, be assured that I am in no way denying Apostolic succession as we normally refer to it, I am simply speaking of yet another, this one communicated by means of eyes and ears rather than the laying on of hands). Perhaps He himself first granted His blessings and His bounteous presence to poor fishermen precisely because they were unable to then sequester themselves and reduce the influence of the Spirit by devoting

Crisis

the world within us? How is a teacher to instruct children or even older students, for that matter, about piety, love, beatitude, or spirit before they have ever seen piety, love, beatitude, or spirit? We can draw a comparison, not with the blind — for surely God could not have created us blind to our inner life — nor with the deaf man who could suddenly hear, for they are more like the poorly instructed child, who hears these words without understanding what they refer to. What, then, do they then imagine when they hear these words?

PRIOR. Well, well, this might cast your ability to teach students in a different light. Anytime you wish you can show school children what you mean by using stories that illustrate the conduct and words of holy men and women.

MONK. I am speaking of our inner life, that from which outer life issues forth. Deeds and words may be the fruits of a pious state of mind, but they might also be an empty illusion. We can never point to a deed and say: this is piety — this is love. One who has already felt true piety, true love, or seen it streaming directly from a pious and loving person, he will understand, he will be able to recognize the same beautiful things in the stories of the saints. But let us imagine someone who has never encountered true piety either in himself or in others, and has only pursued external illusion. Then when his teacher — he too, a man of illusion — lets him read a legend about piety and then explains: 'See, that is piety!' — how can he not comprehend the saint's interior life as being akin to the thoughts and concerns of his instructor? And even if, in spite of everything, a spark of that true piety persisted in the words of the legend and shone through — would he not still run the risk of confusing that dimly glittering spark with the gorgeous, but inauthentic illusion radiating from his teacher? — Or consider one who has never felt true love for Our Savior or his Mother or seen it with his own eyes — if he is taught by a teacher who is equally inexperienced, who feels only the fear of sin all the while referring to this fear as 'love of God' — how can he not then adopt the designations of his teacher, so that he too then imagines 'love of God' to be more a fear of sin than anything else? — And thus it follows that the beautiful

113

Karin Boye

name of one single, internal quality can conceal ten thousand different realities, including ones that contradict the original intention so profoundly that they might be considered the worst adversaries of the original!

Here, at last, I have arrived at what has been so nefariously distorted. I mean, namely, that not even the holiest of scriptures can avoid this fate of being misunderstood according to the nature and experiences of those reading them. Regardless of all the exegesis and explication by church fathers, and the thousands of commentaries ratified by synod after synod, the bare words remain a puzzle the solution to which is held exclusively by those who have actually encountered, in life and spirit, what the words convey.

PRIOR. I am beginning to understand you. And I am beginning at the same time to understand that no nefarious distortion has in fact taken place. This path you have embarked upon, my son, is a dangerous one. Following it would shake the foundations of our faith.

MONK. Far from it, Father! When I say that words alone teach us nothing about what is innermost and highest, what I actually mean is that it's the living spirit, imbued in human form, that can teach us everything! When such a person stands facing another, someone who has yet to experience an act of spirit — that person will perceive it immediately and comprehend. One smile, one gesture of the hand while walking amid the multitudes will teach any and all who see it to understand what it is to love fearlessly — and better than any book in the world could. Spirit ignites spirit, adding link upon link, creating a holy chain through the ages, never broken, unending. This is the true Apostolic succession that began in the days of our Lord Jesus Christ (and please, venerable Father, be assured that I am in no way denying Apostolic succession as we normally refer to it, I am simply speaking of yet another, this one communicated by means of eyes and ears rather than the laying on of hands). Perhaps He himself first granted His blessings and His bounteous presence to poor fishermen precisely because they were unable to then sequester themselves and reduce the influence of the Spirit by devoting their short but invaluable lives to the barren task of writing. Instead, they sowed seeds through their own person, their message making an immediate impact. The effort devoted to transmitting eternal truths clearly and unambiguously may be a joy and a guidance for those who are already wise — but for those who are most in need of instruction, teaching happens not only in words but in the transmission of spirit, with or without words, through the spirit of living people. I would go so far as to say that an uneducated man who radiates spirit, even without ever opening his mouth or being able to differentiate A from B, is an infinitely better instructor than a learned man who teaches about something that neither fills nor possesses him — This is the point I wanted to make! Nothing in any way impious, my Father, but rather, a simple enactment of Scripture: 'Written not with ink, but with the Spirit of the living God.'

PRIOR. I am afraid, truly afraid, that this is all a net laid out by Satan to lure vulnerable souls. I clearly see now where all of this is leading.

MONK. Venerable Father, you're frightening me! The only conclusion I have drawn from my speculations is that if we seek to be true teachers in the holy faith, it's less important for us to read and study than to seek the one essential element and perfect ourselves in piety.

PRIOR. Now allow me to tell you the conclusions that I, and many others too, would draw from your teachings, were they allowed to spread.

First and foremost: if what you say were true, then the church might just as well urge all the school teachers in the land post-haste to teach whatever they wished, whether the dark arts or hedonism, anything, in other words, anything but the tenets of Christianity. For if all that schoolchildren could understand of holy words was what they saw in their teacher — how many of those grumpy, drunken, greedy, lazy teachers would then be deemed worthy of acting as a mediating bridge to the truth? I am well aware that there are also good, conscientious, sober, God-fearing teachers. Let us be generous and say that more than half of them are. But even

Karin Boye

then — how many of those would be worthy? How many men of the church? How many people on earth at all? The only ones who could teach the sacred would be the saints themselves!

MONK. On that matter, I am more confident than you, my Father. For I believe that each person is capable of sharing what he has been given, and no one is so impoverished as to have received nothing from above. When he gives, there will be twelve baskets again. But in one respect I am afraid you are correct, all too correct: if no one can grant knowledge of spiritual life beyond what he himself has inside him, in spirit and truth, then perhaps it is too much to demand that any person teach any of the specific truths of our church. Doing so could lead to the unfortunate consequence that when teaching about God's wrath, he might only be teaching the iniquitous rage of our earthly fathers, and in speaking of God's grace, he might actually just be imparting his own slack capacity for indulgence.

PRIOR. That would be unfortunate indeed, if not something worse. The deeper one immerses oneself in this reasoning, the farther one is led astray. Another dreadful consequence of your thinking occurs to me now (and this alone suffices to show how reprehensible your mediations are): if it were as you say, then one could never be certain which teachings were true. A person might preach the most despicable heresies, the purest heathenism — but as long as he possessed spirit then his listeners would learn more about the Eternal One from him than from listening to someone lacking spirit but who has earnestly attempted to follow the Scripture and the Church Fathers! But that would be absurd.

MONK. I had not thought that far, and what you say now, venerable Father, frightens me more than I can express. Must my thinking really lead to that logical conclusion?

PRIOR. Yes — because your concept of eternal truth is so categorically false. You confuse holiness itself with the experience that humans have of it. You see revelation through the human soul but forget that many things are revealed to us that the human soul will never be capable of grasping. Who is capable of grasping the mystery of the Trinity? No one, not

Crisis

the wisest person on earth! And who would have experience of it? No one, not even the most pious person! Nonetheless, it remains a holy reality, revealed to us through the Word alone: *that is simply how it is!* — It may be incomprehensible or impossible to experience, but that is how it is. That is why the Word grants us knowledge itself, even if no one can even fathom what lies behind it. Such is the mystery of faith!

MONK. Thank you for considering my humble musings so thoroughly. On my own I would never have discovered their snares, but now, in the light of your guidance, I see them clearly.

PRIOR. What I have said thus far will be sufficient, but let me further elaborate upon the horrific conclusions you might have reached had you not been warned in time.

If one were to rely entirely upon what you call spiritual experience, by which you — in your bewilderment — seem to mean that the holy words, teachings, and dogmas are nothing more than the names given to such experience — what assurance would one have that a single God actually existed at all for us, beyond our own narrow souls? If you were to go to the most shackled, earthbound, dissolute, or arrogant of the bondsmen of this world — would not the God that he teaches his children to worship likely bear a great resemblance to what we would call Satan? Examining and approving his teachings through repeated church meetings would help little, if at all — it simply would not matter. For none of his teachings as he expressed them would have anything to do with the Communion of Saints. No book, no writing, no resolution from any synod would any longer suffice to communicate anything about spiritual truths — simply put — *no one would really know who, what, or where God is.* Any attempt to understand holiness beyond what was attainable by individual experience would not be the least bit significant!! A church, a fellowship of the holy, would be entirely impossible (apart from some kind of fellowship beyond human comprehension, knowable only to the angels. Humans themselves would be unable to tell who else belonged to it!). Spiritual teaching would be virtually impossible, for every lesson would run the dangerous risk

Karin Boye

of imparting knowledge about Satan rather than God! Individuals would be utterly abandoned, left on their own, helpless, fumbling through a darkness, black as night — a deep despair would weigh down on humanity. What a colossal heresy! If I were to ask someone: 'What do you know about God?' the reply would be arbitrary, vague, a collection of similes not unlike when a troubadour tries to describe his beloved — and even such a vague response would leave me no more to work with than if the same man had simply remained silent while I observed his character and life! What would stop people from asking: 'What exactly do we need the church for anyway? None of her credos can teach us anything more than we've already learned from the simple people around us. Will we not always need to fear that anything the church does teach us will only deceive us, that her pious words only belie a deeper impiety? Is it not the case that no matter how you look at them — pious or not — words only teach us about the human uttering them!' — Your thinking leads to the dreadful conclusion that *any doctrine about God, piety or the highest of virtues is impossible.*

MONK. Father, Father, this shakes me to my core. I tremble from head to toe! To which saint shall I offer my gratitude and blessings — surely the holy Thomas Aquinas, his guidance no doubt led you here and granted you the power to persuade a misguided son. Impose penance on me, my Father, for the arrogant recklessness of listening to my own, unexamined thoughts in this way! And above all: please speak on my behalf to my revered abbot so that for the time being, for my soul's improvement, he might spare me from the kind of work that allows my thoughts to wander idly upon everything from Earth to Heaven and thereby fall too easily into the snares of Hell! Work that demands my full attention might save my soul! I am so afraid, I tremble like a sleepwalker who has awakened to find himself at the edge of an abyss!

Crisis

Malin had been summoned to the Principal's office.

How can anyone know how often they've sinned? She could be guilty of anything. There were countless opportunities for grave offenses: at home, in school, at the teachers' college — wrongs of which you remained oblivious until you received your punishment. Malin wracked her brain trying to think of any clear sins of commission or omission, but found none. There was no point to it anyway — you could feel anxious about a thing, but it was almost always something else. Regardless of whether she could recall any particular wrongdoing, her conscience couldn't be considered clear by any stretch of the imagination — and this affected everything, even tangible, everyday matters like whether her daily work met the minimum requirements. Or it might be nothing to do with her work. The college was not exclusively, and perhaps not even primarily, an institution for vocational training; moral education was equally important. Morality was central to the vocation, it went along with the job, you could say. Malin was deeply conscious of the fact that her present state of mind left much to be desired — her facial expressions and tone of voice inevitably conveyed this when she least wished it or was aware of it. There was no corner of the soul that remained entirely private, nowhere she had the right to say: this concerns only me and no one else. At least not if you're a teacher, or going to be one. Sooner or later all things are made manifest by the light, *liber scriptus proferetur.*

If only she could stay calm, and *not start crying.* That only made things worse. She clenched her fists vigorously as she plodded down the wide, bright hallway.

Karin Boye

The Principal sat at her desk, absorbed in a ledger. She had the remarkable capacity to focus all of the intense energy her seemingly delicate little person could muster on whatever matter lay at hand. That's why she was a prodigious worker and a great organizational talent. The Principal's sharp brown eyes hovered in fascination over the columns of the ledger, giving Malin the impression that she and the Principal were in two different rooms. After a couple of minutes, the ledger was slammed shut and pushed to a desk corner where it no longer existed. The Principal was utterly present with Malin and nowhere else. The overpowering strength of her will filled the room like an electric current.

'Would you please take a seat!'

In other words, this would take a while. Well, what else did she expect, with such a ceremonious summons to report to the Principal's office at a precise time.

'What do you plan to do after your studies here?'

An explosion! It was the last thing she had anticipated. She sat paralyzed with dismay at such an ordinary, natural question.

She ought to have given the only possible, only imaginable response:

'I'm going to be an elementary school teacher.' Instead, she sat completely silent, aghast as if at some scandalous revelation.

Her path had seemed so clear to her. Naturally, she had wanted to be an elementary school teacher, that's why she was here! It simply hadn't occurred to her that there might be another path besides becoming a teacher. The children were living material, growing souls to be guided along the same paths where she herself had found peace and strength. She had several reasons for wanting to work in an elementary school. One was simply that it afforded greater possibility to influence students in a profound way. Teaching a single subject in a private high school, going from class to class, would mean that the children would always see her as one of a dozen constantly changing, more or less unfamiliar, figures — but an elementary school teacher teaching all subjects to the same class, and following them over the years, would become an exceptional figure to the children, with an influence rivaled only by their parents. Another reason was that she wanted to work with the people — yes, the people without quotation marks, because they *were* the people, they were the actual, ordinary people, with whom she had to feel at home, because all she desired was to be real and ordinary, a simple person among simple people, one of millions — this had always been her ambition, from as far back as her schooldays, when out of disgust for the snobbish aesthetes around her she had confessed: 'Sure, I'm a philistine, but that's all I ever want to be!' — She wanted to be a stone in the foundation, a person not weighed down by any superior demand to be exceptional, but rather one who fulfilled her small duties faithfully and well. The future appeared before her in the enticing image of a rainy street in a large city, at daybreak in the autumn — a path made up of work and celebrating the everyday. In other words: the life-adventure of an elementary school teacher.

She ought to have responded quickly and confidently. That's what was expected of her. But she remained silent, paralyzed and exposed.

She imagined herself standing before a class teaching the eternal truths. Laying the foundations upon which the children's first religious and ethical concepts would be built...

Malin's silence took the Principal by surprise. What had come over the girl? Hadn't she given any thought at all to the future? Only students could be such strangers to the way the world worked. Or perhaps her dreams were much loftier? Or was she secretly engaged? — so many of the most gifted ones had been plucked that way, just as they were blossoming! In one sense it was lamentable, in another, completely natural, and there was nothing much to be done about it.

'Do you not know what you want to be, Fröken Forst?' She asked, with a hint of sarcasm.

'Well yes — a teacher.'

I hope that's the truth, the Principal thought to herself, knowing full well that she was the last one they told when they got engaged, not before it was made public. But there

Karin Boye

were always telltale signs that those who knew what to look for could see. It took half a second for the Principal's quick brown eyes to assess Malin's appearance and come to the reassuring conclusion: not engaged, positively not.

Institutions were Principal Melling's creative medium without a doubt, and she fervently devoted her organizational talents to rejuvenating them. Had she been a man she might have chosen a career in politics and become a great, successful politician, that is, unless her strong ethical principles had propelled her toward education anyway. As it was, she was as much the teachers' college's politician as its Principal. At once diminutive, tough, and nimble as quicksilver, she had finally worked her way up to a position of power where she had the space to put her unique character to use. Her more contemplative work at the college, such as morning prayers and scripture lessons constituted, in a sense, the tender heart within her otherwise largely extroverted life: this was the seed from which life springs — just as her unsentimental and level-headed piety dictated the ultimate goals of her numerous other endeavors. Principal Melling oriented herself to an inner map that was as different from Malin's as a minister's is from a hermit's.

Of the graduating class at the college, Malin Forst was the student who interested her most, not in terms of personality, but talent. Her personality was altogether too malleable, altogether too feminine — too feminine for Principal Melling to be entirely content with it. Her own bitter experience had taught her that a woman not only had to be two or even three times superior to her male competitors for any of her own ideas to make it to the starting line, but her skin had to be much thicker than a man's need be. There was nothing to be done about it; you had to be content with what you were given and hope for mercy in life — anyway, a few would be spared; 'God tempers the wind to the shorn lamb,' as the saying went. Talent, on the other hand, was paramount, and should be taken seriously. For the common good, something more must be made out of Malin than a little elementary school teacher sent to the back of beyond.

Crisis

And so, she continued:

'Have you ever thought about continuing your studies?'

An expression of indecision crossed Malin's face. Had that occurred to her? It had crossed her mind at some point, although hardly as a definite plan or intention. Having an advanced degree would save her from having to teach Christianity in elementary school. But it was more than that. She longed for knowledge. Not the knowledge acquired in school, but another kind. Did she want to study philosophy? Or psychology? Yes, more than anything else, psychology. It was strange to think of graduating with facts pounded into one's memory: the year that Fredrik I died or the height of Mont Blanc, while not learning anything at all about the forces that transform one's interior into chaos or cosmos.

'Haven't you ever thought about studying theology?'

'No — not theology.'

How was it possible for someone to be so unaware either of her potential or of her proper place? Principal Melling had an excellent memory and kept track of each and every one of her many students. She knew, therefore, that Malin had chosen to write her graduation exam in high school on a biblical subject and that it had been decidedly above average. Throughout her entire career at the teachers' college Malin had almost exclusively chosen subjects that were either explicitly religious or which at the very least dealt in some way with what it meant to lead a pious life. The deciding factor, of course, was the high quality of the work. Malin's performance on her exam a few days earlier, on which she wrote a more than satisfactory pedagogical analysis of the prophet Jeremiah, had prompted the Principal to initiate this conversation.

On the other hand, Malin's talent for practical tasks was less than zero. As the home economics teacher once put it:

'I can't understand it, Malin Forst doesn't otherwise strike you as unintelligent, but she seems to destroy anything you put in her hands.'

The sewing teacher had expressed the same idea even less tactfully.

123

Karin Boye

At least there would be no risk of such fields luring her away. And even if she were eventually to marry she would be all the more inclined to hire domestic help so as to devote herself entirely to intellectual pursuits.

It could also be the case that Malin Forst had never encountered any real opportunity to develop in any serious way the interests that lay closest to her heart, and consequently never let her thoughts soar as high as studying theology at the university. Her imagination and reason had yet to be set in motion.

So the Principal set about explaining the need for female theologians and teachers of religious pedagogy at women's colleges. There was currently a shortage, which meant that even women's teaching colleges had been forced to hire male instructors in scripture. This practice had significant downsides, the most important being that male instructors could never cultivate the deeper relationships with their students that their female counterparts could. Women thought and reacted differently from men, that's just the way things were.

Naturally, Malin understood that that must be the case?

'I believe that you would be extremely well suited both for theological studies and for a position instructing at a teachers' college,' said the Principal.

Study theology and then teach at a college! The connection was becoming clearer to her. That's why she had been called in!

An immense fury began to boil inside her. Because she had supposedly shown herself to be intelligent? That was what they cared about! But the one truly essential thing? What was more important than talent or intelligence? No one ever asked about that! Everyone simply assumed that she was sufficient on that account! For an instant Malin shook with the rage of a naïve person when she realizes for the first time that a price can be put on honor and integrity. This mundane system of measurement was so infinitely inadequate that people asked whether you had good grades or the ability to write when actually, the wellbeing of people's souls hung in the balance!

Crisis

In the next instant, her rage lashed back at her. Small wonder that they saw her as a pious Christian, considering the hypocrisy she committed every single day here! Whose fault was it actually that no one had thought to inquire about her spirituality? Her own! She went around spouting nonsense exactly as she always had, writing her essays, and teaching her lessons, the whole time slipping from belief to doubt. No one noticed and she hadn't said a word about it. How she despised that cowardly hypocrite, Malin Forst! It was high time that she made her confession!

Quickly and concisely — yes — but how?

'I don't think I'm good enough for that!' she said in a dark tone.

Principal Melling locked eyes with her, at once teasing and amiable.

'And just why wouldn't you be good enough, when there are so many stupid men who are?!'

'That's not what I meant. I'm not good enough — in another sense. Everything has changed recently. I've begun to doubt everything.'

The Principal shook her head dismissively.

'We all go through such phases, Fröken Forst. They are to be taken with a grain of salt. We simply get through them and become even more certain afterward.'

The secure warmth of conviction in her voice didn't reach Malin. Getting through it, after all, was what Principal Melling had experienced. But that's not *always* how it went, you didn't always come out on the other side. And even if you did — how long would it take? Surely it made no sense for her to embark on theology studies in abhorrence and agitation, merely hoping it would all pass?

The silence between them lingered. The Principal expected Malin to speak, to raise her inner concerns, or perhaps start to discuss the practical question of continuing her studies. In the meantime, the Principal gripped a letter opener in her hand and pressed its pliant blade firmly against the tabletop, as if the lassitude of the moment were tormenting her and she could hasten an end to it. Malin saw this motion and misinterpreted it. She too found the silence acute and oppressive, imagining that the Principal had wanted a decisive answer from her. One — two — and forward march! To her it felt as if she had to set her own plan alongside this one and then defend it against the superior will.

'I want to study — psychology!' she blurted out. 'And pedagogy too!' she quickly added, in the hopes that at least *that* would be amenable to the Principal of a teachers' college.

'You do realize that psychology is not a subject worthy of study,' the Principal replied dryly. 'I know, I've done it myself.'

Principal Melling looked back on her time at the university with a certain contempt. The morning lectures on a pedagogy handbook that was objectively inaccurate. And the psychology! Even at the time she had known substantially more about psychology than any of her professors, the only difference being that her knowledge was unsystematic but useful, while theirs was systematic but useless. The psychology experiments brought happiness to no human being; they were exclusively for future researchers experimenting with the psychology of the mind. Supposedly they learned the scientific method... Sure, that was true — but broadly speaking, the ones who could think had already learned to do so before they arrived, and those who couldn't weren't likely to learn to do so in a psychology seminar. The child sitting in front of her expected great things from those wise professors! It was nonsense, pure and simple.

Malin knew nothing about the university other than that it was the highest educational institution and ought to be where the latest scientific findings could be found. It was possible that science hadn't advanced very far in the field of psychology. She harbored no illusions, in fact, about the depth of knowledge it could offer. She had taken psychology classes in high school which dealt with thinking, feeling, and the will; as well as visual, auditory, and tactile-kinesthetic modes of cognition, thank-you very much. But even if all the university did was provide access to bibliographies and methodologies — wouldn't that perhaps be enough to uncover some single, little thread to lead you forward? A bit closer to knowledge

Crisis

that might shield us from a living death? Knowledge that might ward off the surging attacks of chaos?

'Do you really believe that you would do more good in psychology?' the Principal asked. Her voice revealing how abominably stupid she thought it would be to answer yes.

Malin didn't exactly answer in the affirmative:

'Maybe because I'm interested in pursuing it — it could be my true calling —'

The Principal's face darkened into a severe expression. How could it be that a human being could position herself in the great battle on such vague grounds? Was she so utterly devoid of a sense of responsibility for her gifts or for the greater good?

'My dear Fröken Forst,' she said, 'that kind of reasoning is what I call childish and egotistical. We find our *calling* where we are needed, not where we're "interested" in pursuing it!'

Judgment! Scathing judgment! Childish and egotistical! Malin was flooded with shame and guilt, but she couldn't submit and didn't want to! Though the loathsome, hateful tears again began to fall.

The Principal was fairly accustomed to hysterical outbursts. Girls at that age were predisposed to them. They were a direct consequence of families who still treated them as children who, when it came to it, could still get their way by resorting to such tactics. They hadn't yet adapted to the hard reality, the truth that awaited them beyond those protective walls. They didn't necessarily have to be of bad character or especially oversensitive to resort to blubbering — it was simply a residue of childhood. As soon as they realized that tears would get them nowhere, they quickly disappeared.

Partly to distract Malin, Principal Melling inquired, calmly and patiently:

'Well then, Fröken Forst, you never said what you'd like to do with your psychology and pedagogy.'

Her soothing voice didn't stem Malin's flood of tears, quite the opposite, though now she was moved to tears out of gratitude. The Principal was her ally after all, an ally, whom, given her own impudent defiance, she didn't rightly deserve.

Karin Boye

Her resistance abated, her obstinate, selfish pride abated in an impulse of capitulation to submit just as she was. She looked up with a faint smile, swallowing her tears:

'Sometimes I wish there were — a new kind of school — an experimental school — with new methods — — —'

The Principal sat speechless for a moment, struck by the naïveté of the statement. Did the twenty-year-old child sitting before her actually believe that whatever she reached for would land in her lap, simply because she had 'wished for it'? Could she really be that out of touch with the day-to-day struggle for bread, with the fact that most people had to be content with an occupation that met their basic needs and so few ever attained anything beyond that?

Speaking in a quiet, cold voice she awakened the sleeping girl to the realities of the world:

'Fröken Forst, do you perhaps have some private fortune with which to fund such plans?'

A well-placed thrust of the sword into one who had already capitulated! Malin's weeping intensified. It was neither the uncertainty of her future prospects nor the difficulties an impoverished reformer in education would certainly face that overwhelmed her. It was the piercing stab of irony, and the contempt that accompanied it, along with the feeling of being profoundly disadvantaged in her struggle with the Principal, who not only knew her own goals, but in all certainty those of others as well — and herself, who still knew nothing, not the least little thing. All she knew was that she was fumbling along alone, and had to feel her own way as she went.

The Principal nodded, a sign that their conversation had concluded, and Malin slunk away into a far corner of the empty corridor. There she sat down, sobbing.

The small, mundane feeling of shame she felt at behaving thoughtlessly and responding in such a silly, infantile way was almost entirely engulfed by pangs of remorse. We find our *calling* where we are needed, not in what we are 'interested' in pursuing! — childish and egotistical — and then all the Principal's bitter irony, which she more than deserved after reciprocating such kindness, such undeserved friendliness, with clumsy, blind, unkindness... Your calling awaits you... There it was again, the demand that she didn't want to follow, because she was too egoistical, too I-centered, an apostate, in other words, of the Only True Will.

But deep within her, as if deep in the cellar, a sleepwalker began to stir, someone who no longer concerned herself with how much crying she heard far above, not anymore — it was someone who had begun to feel confident because there was no longer any option not to. Even had she been commanded a hundred times to obey, a hundred times she would have had to turn away. Right or wrong — there's something called necessity. My necessity. My will!

The tears slowly ceased flowing, and the sleepwalker expanded to dwell in the entirety of her being.

The calm of accepting the unavoidable. The calm of inner fate.

Had she at last whole-heartedly embraced the side of the eternal dissenters, in the face of duty and commandment and law and morals? Possibly. A meager light flickered through the darkness, whether a star or a will-o'-the-wisp was uncertain. Consciousness: this is me; this is mine.

You severe and alien force, I am just as you are. I, too, am sword and will.

Karin Boye

'So, you believe that I'm retreating so quickly!' said the Principal, laying her little hand assuredly upon conscience's long meeting table of celestial emerald. 'Quite the contrary, I'm staying precisely where I am.'

Even here, in the Assembly of the Highest Ones, neither peace nor harmony reigned. They bickered, their withering glances of icy disdain blanching each other to shadows. At their most civil, one adversary might propose subsuming an esteemed opponent and thus proffer him a kind of extended life, as a valuable part of a larger whole, with continuity preserved.

For a High One, however, it was exceedingly embarrassing to feel one's boundaries and dignity begin to soften. It was only natural that the Principal resisted, sensing the threat to her was serious.

The one she turned toward was a gentleman, a newcomer by all appearances. As such he conducted himself with the impudence, not the shyness, of a newcomer. The faces of the other assembly members clearly read, 'He has no business here!' Yet he had been let in, and there he stood.

'Sir, by what right do you address this assembly?' The Principal had regained the floor. 'Look around you and be ashamed! Do not for one second believe that I am speaking on behalf of my earthly namesake, who, though an esteemed and reputable person, is still rather ephemeral from the perspective of eternity. I make no claim to hold the keys to enslaving or liberating the spirit in my weak, mortal hands. That would be arrogant. But everyone, no matter how inconsequential or exceptional, no matter where they stand,

Crisis

represents power and sovereignty. I am not alone! I would even dare say that I stand before you, a representative of the more valuable part of humanity — more valuable, sir, take note!'

She lifted her hand, and figures closed in around her, forming a shield of sentries. Right by her side: well-known functionaries from the Christian summer rallies where echoes of 'The Church of our Fathers' rang out in the open air, transforming each and every one into a foot soldier. And alongside them the leaders of evening congregations where people gathered to debate existential questions and one seemed to glimpse the centuries-long struggle of the pious that illuminated the present, making it visible, as the winter darkness outside the window reflected flames burning as the bright faces of angels, faces burning with the flame of spirit. The holy ones in checkered cotton dresses! The holy ones in black blazers of Cheviot wool! And behind them: those of a bygone era who had shared the same struggle and been laid to rest. As they flocked to surround the Principal where she stood, steadfast and ardent, their inner radiance swelled forth from its sheath, extending in all directions until they all stood, enveloped in dazzling white illumination, the white illumination come into being through great misery. The millions of All Saints Day candles blazed together to commemorate the daily struggle. The endless procession of siblinghood bridging the ages mercifully engulfed each and every one in its mighty flow. All Saints Day hymns of victory and longing resounded over them all. All Saints! Amen! Amen!

The Principal held up her other hand and the spectacle withdrew in pale eddies of incense.

'I am all of this,' she said. 'Metaphorically, and also in the situation as it is now. Good sir, I stand before you and this assembly as the authorized representative of God. Once more I ask you: by what right do you seek to address this assembly — the blossom of the ages?'

The newcomer shook his head of blue-black hair. Drops of burning venom splattered around him.

'By the right of despair,' he answered.

Karin Boye

They booed and shouted, less at the words he had uttered than at something worse: the trembling metallic peal of his voice seemed blasphemous, it reminded them too much of —
— —

As he lifted his heavy eyelids they saw that his gaze had grown mighty. He had gathered powers in the depths of his eye while exiled in the outermost reaches of darkness. There was no need for power there.

'By the power of eternal resurrection!'

He wrapped his pliant, iridescent hands around the hilt of a sword that shot lightning bolts as it whipped back and forth — everyone could see he was armed to the teeth and could hear that he resounded with the clinking of metal —

'By the power of lineage and kin!'

Everyone's eyes shifted timidly along the immense meeting table, like walking and walking and walking along the corridor of a dream. A long way above them, the far end of the table disappeared in a primeval mist. Like hazy mountains at dawn, the oldest and most powerful ones were barely discernible there, motionless. Occasionally they whispered to one another and the sound of their voices, like the sigh of a metallic wind, reached the younger assembly members where they sat, closer to the door, closer to the ruckus of the present day...

A small man in simple, even ragged medieval clothing stood up at his place to speak. It wasn't Meister Eckhart, for his attire was earthly, but rather a cousin of the great mystic, a Protestant cousin, who held a greater sense of the weight of personality than his relative. He had been a man working in some kind of craft or profession, perhaps a cobbler like Böhme, or an elementary school teacher, who knows.

'That was Lucifer who just addressed us!' he said. 'The evil spirit, that original renegade himself, has spoken to us. Do you really intend to grant him a place at our meeting? His path leads away from obedience.'

'Are you referring to me?' said the newcomer. 'It is true that my path leads away from obedience. But if the assembly would

Crisis

be so good as to look in this direction, I will demonstrate that I am far from alone on this path.'

At a snap of his fingers the air around him blackened with riotous battle. An army of distorted features materialized: shrunken figures, slaves with filthy faces, slaves with crooked backs, impotent hatred, impotent disdain. Thersites's ridiculous form hobbled forth spewing ugly words that hung from the corners of his mouth like toad-feet and rat-tails. All of the ugly and lowly, who howl into darkness with envy, everything that has been kicked, and seeks with a slither and a hiss to strike the heel of the foot that dealt the blow.

The assembly sat in silent repulsion.

From out of the dark mass of subhuman life, figures bolted forth to live for an instant and then perish again. Like a pack of skulking wolves, Spartacus's legions closed in around him, scrambling out of ditches and ravines, rising up, the long rows of their crosses visible against the night sky. Fires glimmered forth. Heretics and blasphemers with glass beakers and compasses devoted themselves to forbidden research. — Galileo on his knees to recant his teachings. — Giordano Bruno at the stake.

The assembly grew agitated.

A man with a beard and a cloak demanded the floor. It seemed to be the prophet Jeremiah, he too imprisoned in his day for high treason. Or perhaps it was Amos, the shepherd from Tekoa, who became enraged that the poor could be sold for a pair of sandals. It's not always easy to tell people apart in such an immense group whose members are so inclined to amalgamation.

'But aren't we familiar with all this as well?' he said. 'Why do you wish to claim it as exclusively yours? It's true, they fight on their own behalf, and true as well that they have yet to be embraced by the communion of saints — but haven't many of us also experienced this during our lives struggling on earth? What is the difference between you and us?'

Lucifer shrugged his shoulders.

'*I am* not the one to ask about that! A matter of tradition, I suppose?' he replied nonchalantly.

Karin Boye

At a toss of his head, the smoky black air turned a deeper and deeper blue, becoming a blue, blue sea, across which swarms of tiny sails could be seen toiling slowly towards the unknown like foolhardy insects: Egyptian feluccas with leather wings, purple sails, Tyrian and Hellenic. The high prow of a Spanish *nave* glided forth as if in a dream, past sunsets and sunrises, nighttime seas and daytime seas like a fixed, never flinching stare. It appeared to grow larger, closer and closer. At the prow stood Columbus, squinting into the wind. He was surveying new land, but the new land he glimpsed rose out of the water not as coastlines and islands, but rather in the form of undulating, expectant human fates: the smiles of ten thousand kinds of happiness alongside ten thousand sighs of as many different misfortunes. Ten thousand souls' mines and ore waiting to be discovered and named. Ten thousand possibilities, yet unborn, to form a life.

The host of fates grew still and cleared as the tens of thousands dissolved together, finding repose in a single face, a fine, strict face, in which all lines culminated in a tranquil hymn.

'We'll cast anchor here for the time being,' said Columbus, descending from the ship. And the assembly saw that it was just Lucifer amusing himself by donning a little disguise to throw dust in their eyes. He still led his most recent candidate for apotheosis by the hand.

Marcus Aurelius and Buddha exchanged glances — each found himself in a relatively faded state in the assembly and was thus open to the possibility of respectable assimilation — and nodded. The new candidate possessed a certain distinguished nobility that they found appealing.

From a more distant part of the table a small, lithe, brown figure glided forward. So he was still alive! It had been such a long time since his voice had been heard in the assembly. The eyes of several more current members of the assembly widened, and the mouth of Meister Eckhart's cousin, which otherwise emoted such heavenly goodness, twisted into a rather nasty sneer. The lithe figure's chest was bare, revealing his totem, tattooed in blue: The Turtle. It was Uncas, the last

Crisis

of the Mohicans, who in his day — though quite a while ago now — had been a great power in the assembly of advisors.

'At last!' he said. 'At last, a human of noble lineage, of the noble tribe of Human! Noble in and of itself. Human by pride and virtue, even if no one else welcomes you — I, though a mere shadow of the past, receive you, I Uncas. Hmph! I have spoken.'

Several of the more recent holy ones possessed a certain sympathy for the diminutive brown warrior and considered themselves more or less distantly related to him. Saint George the dragon slayer — whose smooth, youthful forehead displayed the charm and luster of the joy that accompanies imminent victory — held nothing against Uncas, truly, aside from the fact that he had fought on his own account rather than as the designated swain of the Queen of Heaven. On that matter, the saint knew for certain that the great body of white stood on his side. The new candidate behind Lucifer struck him as similarly unsympathetic. Though she certainly could have looked more repulsive — she did possess a basic dignity.

Fröken Mogren stood up at the lower end of the table and, citing Viktor Rydberg ('He is to be found in the one, who does not receive His name') demanded the floor:

'The name has nothing to do with the issue. Why should those of us gathered here, the Principal, and Eckhart's cousin, and I, along with the thousands of others, not welcome a pure, aspiring and idealistic figure as a sister and equal in the great body of white? What business has Lucifer with her?'

At that the rebellious figure emitted a diabolical laugh as unpleasant as a public information film.

'May I remind you, ladies and gentlemen, that it is the power I hold, that opened these doors for *my* candidate, raising her up to heights such as these. Might the assembly perhaps be willing to acknowledge this power as legitimate ...?'

A murmur of displeasure swept through the ones in white. One simply didn't mention such things, it was tasteless, we have heard more than enough such talk in our days. The silence of their initial moral revulsion was then shattered once again by shouting and booing. This time the noise was deafening.

Lucifer smiled inscrutably. The age-old battle was already back in full swing, waged not with earthly weapons but with the arcane forces that arouse and nourish ideals only to slay them when their time is up. He stood there, a dark general among embattled warriors and smiled — hopelessly, as the eternally rebellious figure does, conscious of never being able to triumph completely so long as he remains who he is — and yet full of hope, as the lord of eternal renewal, conscious that he can never be completely vanquished, as long as life is lived.

Crisis

At what miraculous threshold did profound meaning become form, in line and movement?

At the same miraculous threshold where light became light and sound became sound. At the pregnant threshold of infatuation.

The one-celled protozoan with its lone, shadowy sense drifted monotonously through the darkness until gripped by oceanic infatuation. Thus, the ocean came into being by developing a sense of feeling; hydrogen-oxygen molecules became meaningful — and sweet, fresh coolness entered into the world. Gripped then by infatuation with the vastness of space, it created reverberant expanses and with it, the sense of hearing; waves of air became meaningful — and murmurs and sound entered into the world. Then, gripped by cosmic infatuation, it engendered the luminous universe and with it the sense of sight, so that vibrations in the ether became meaningful — and color and light entered into the world. Eternal love created a world aligned to its purpose.

One day, sight, who spoke uneasily, as one who is constantly observing must, remarked:

'I'm confused. I no longer know whether I am sight or not. I envelop things and follow them as if I were touch, I hold my breath in quiet anticipation as if I were hearing, I breathe in, like one intoxicated, as if I were smell, and I drink in long, deep draughts as if I were taste. One thing I do know: profound meaning lies in all that I envelop, hear, breathe, and drink, meaning toward which I grope with dread. Could I be standing at the threshold of some new creation?'

Karin Boye

Hearing answered softly, as one who is constantly listening must:

'I know, I know! When music takes possession of me it's not the clarity or tone of individual sounds that makes me happy, and neither is it how the synthesis of a chord caresses the senses. What I seek in the notes is something lying beneath and beyond them. Tell me, sister sight: can a rich purple or the dazzling play of light fill you with life as fully as that enigma you speak of — the human lines and movements that reveal a new world? Admit it — isn't revelation through the senses at the same time the revelation of what lies beyond the senses, of what creates the senses, of the limitless feelings of eternal love? Is it not the mirage of a kingdom in the process of creation?'

'Even I, the least of the brothers,' said taste, 'can be gripped by the intoxication of such equivalence: a single drop of bitterness, a single drop of acidity can hit me as if it were a call to victory — as a reminder of the organism's elastic oscillations before it leaps. And how much more you, then, my more expansive siblings, how much more you must then be able to pursue the equivalence between the senses and the inner anticipation of the leap, and flight!'

Crisis

Filled with shy reverence, Malin awoke to new days, on an entirely new plane of reality. Objects in the material world had taken on a deep hue and new proximity, they summoned and enthralled her. Even the road from the station to the college every morning became a perplexing adventure, the morning rays of the spring sun shone upon the rooftops of the apartment blocks, revealing a world of deep warmth and clarity replete with meaning more immense than words could convey. It was as if every glimmer and glint of daylight drew near with a sudden, barely perceptible and quickly evaporating floral scent, a fragrance full of that soft and secretive organic life with which baskets of roses brimmed. She held her breath, her heart stilled, as she tried to capture the instant, ethereal promise in their scent.

The adventure she experienced on the road only anticipated the greater one that followed: the ceremonious first encounter of the day. Every time she saw her was like resting again in that profound stillness. It was so effacingly beautiful — she could never quite fix it in her mind. Even the most beautiful of recollections was impotent in the face of reality — it made no difference that she lived from day to day, by and for and in and through these encounters. It was like living to perform altar duties, living in pursuit of something both sacred and formidable.

Formidable — in that Siv was more than just Siv, she was the revelation of a new life course. An ivory neck rising above perfectly sloping shoulders can place more direct demands on one's conduct without uttering a word, more than all of the commandments put together.

Karin Boye

To Malin it felt as if the semi-melting spine within her were contracting in a spasm that was painful yet somehow beneficial, born of a thirst for restraint and resilience. The imperative power that she had so vainly solicited was present within her.

No one could have been more oblivious to all of this than Siv. The quick glances that gave Malin such strength were imperceptible to everyone else. She never deliberately had to go searching for Siv, they ran into each other often enough, in the hallways, on the stairs, in the classroom; and the asceticism intrinsic to receiving each fleeting encounter as a gift granted by the moment played into the tough but delectable self-education that Siv unwittingly demanded. In Malin's eyes, attempting to force a person like Siv to endure her company would have constituted a vulgar ingratitude: you've received the gift of new life and the splendors of Earth and Heaven alike — and yet you crave still more? But there was a selfish timidity in her restraint as well: now that she enjoyed happily consigning herself, whether in grace or disgrace, to an unknown course of events within her, she backed away, perhaps so as not to disturb its reverence and authenticity with some false step, or sentimental inflection, or with one of the many other elements of inauthenticity still strewn about, remnants of her time of sickness that were still to be surmounted. She preferred to wait and let forces do their work. The words that she and Siv did exchange were few and mundane. This too coalesced with the image of Siv and the pathway that Siv was. The more intently mundane, the more Siv.

For Siv was allied with immediate, certain, and self-evident existence, with tangible objects as well as mute creatures, animals and plants. To Malin, who approached her from without, with her eyes rather than through any spiritual connection, she seemed more like a flower than a battling soul. That was an exaggeration, of course, the consequence of Malin not knowing Siv in any other way. *More* or *less*, however, in that something about Siv's bearing and nature set her apart from the others. It was a bearing and nature that drew the

Crisis

gaze outward in a different way. Ever since spring had arrived, and so incredibly early that year — with an April as warm as summer — Malin discovered a change in her relationship to life that existed aside from words. She had always sought isolation and nature, but had largely seen events of the natural world — budding, blossoming and pollination, sprouting and wilting — symbolically, as a stepping stone into some interior, sacred world. Now, when she held a leaf bud or picked a blade of grass, her hand touched the smooth surface of a yet-unknown and scarcely knowable *you*, gold-green with the seething life of the sun, something she never could have grasped through her own narrow human experience. A *you*, happily self-contained, aligned with its essence and demanding nothing beyond it, remaining all the while — despite its insurmountable limits — a source of exuberant joy and life for the strange being who stood there, merely grazing its surface. Riding the train to and from the city she would wait on the platform, quivering with the delight of discerning leaves and bright shoots as they developed. Yes, Siv was of them. She grew as they did, in the assurance of that secret, immanent law of the root. That is how she had grown as beautiful as a young tree or a flower.

But what must it have taken for a human being to remain so unscathed?

Her blood and nerves still pulsing with the memory of chaos, Malin regarded a person living in harmony as a delicate water lily floating on a sea of disturbing and destructive influences. Its only feeble chance of life was to feel its way forward — at once cautiously and boldly — according to the measure of its own essence, and then maintain this position through strict discipline. All the discipline of elasticity and flexibility, rhythm and movement that imbues swimmers and dancers with power to demonstrate the freest kind of constraint — Siv was all of this. Everything that proudly and naturally subordinated itself to its own necessity, and let it bear the fullness of holy blossoms that can develop with each new exigency. Malin held secret and devoted meetings with Siv in the showers at the college, not in person, but with Siv as type, taking the form of cold showers twice daily. These lasted

Karin Boye

not a second longer than necessary to serve their purpose — this too according to the type.

There were relapses, some more noticeable to the outside world than others. It's not as if passing from the sickness she had embodied into the health that Siv embodied would happen at the flick of a switch. But Malin's relapses neither discouraged nor disheartened her, for labor and sacrifice in the cause of great devotion filled her with the elation of conquest.

One of the most difficult setbacks came one day when class met in the gymnasium.

Malin was not a distinguished gymnast by any stretch of the imagination. Her strengths lay elsewhere. And now that the body in all of its wondrous splendor had presented itself to her as a revelation of life, she found her own lack of athleticism even more lamentable. She would gladly have traded some of her talent for essay writing to be even slightly better on the pommel horse. Only with patience and practice would she achieve that goal.

One thing she was hopeless at was rope climbing. When Fröken Tybb let the ropes down and Siv and Malin each took their place beside one, a shiver passed through Malin, more from wonder than fright: would she, in the new state of being that she now found herself, be able to accomplish feats that had been impossible before? Why not? Why not believe in such a miracle — especially one so small and insignificant compared to the magnificent ones that had already inundated her?

An initial exertion — unsuccessful. Then again — and again — still nothing. One more try — Siv was already high above her — it has to work — such a detestable, doughy lump of a body — detestable mush for muscles — detestable detestable, revolting little shrimp that can't even climb — — — It has to work, but it doesn't, it's not working, not working — — —

Energy seeped over into rage that culminated in a hysterical breakdown. Fröken Tybb waved Nanni Fransson over, saying:

'Take her out into the corridor and calm her down!'

Crisis

Crushed, Malin sat beside Nanni Fransson, oblivious to her attempts at comfort. Something deep within her was working intensely. This was a defeat. Not because she failed to reach the top, but rather in that she had taken such insignificant child's play as significant. She had sinned against what in actuality was most significant. She had violated the state of being, by which you remain composed and calm in the face of facts — whether they show themselves kind or unkind. Or put another way: sinned against Siv.

And thus, as Nanni Fransson sat trying to calm her, Malin, still oblivious to her efforts, forced her way inward, not only through her hysterical vanity and an equally hysterical self-loathing, but also through the shame of it all, even deeper into knowing the principle that was Siv. From bitterness: honey; from defeat: victory. If she was to feel ashamed in front of Siv, even wildly ashamed — then so be it. Through and through! And even if Siv despised her — then that would be right as well, she could do what she had to do. Malin would just renew her exertions and compel Siv to respect her — and it didn't matter if Siv, the human being who couldn't see inside her or have knowledge of everything that had happened, were to deny her — she would still embrace everything that Siv represented, everything she expressed...

After that day, she never had an overt outburst again.

Everything that Siv expressed...

It was not through words or conversation, nor anything that any common language would refer to as the soul, that she had perceived the message with which everything had changed; it was through lines and movement alone. Yet this knowledge was clear, far from enigmatic, and less ambiguous than words would have been. Malin was learning a new language: the language of material objects. It nearly replaced the well-known system of names and concepts that she had either cast off or lost at the edge of this endless expanse. She fumbled and spelled her way forward into this novelty. Seeking some resemblance to her own situation, her mind returned again and again to a mysterious painting she had once seen reproduced: a naked child lies alone, wide-eyed on the savannah; on the horizon, morning clouds recede behind curious trees as strange animals drink from pools or graze on the wide plain; the child lies silent and still, its eyes full of an unknown day. — Thus she now stood, in the presence of things.

They were so immediate, so proximate, and spoke neither in allegory nor with any intermediary translation of concepts. Utterly and fundamentally singular, they cast themselves upon her. Her senses were bombarded from every direction by these immediate impulses, both of action and attitude, against which she had to defend herself, saying no and yes.

Some things were so dangerous that she had to drive them away. Dusk things. Moonlight things. The treacherous paintings, poems, music that tempted one to relinquish all sense and self-control and sink back into chaos, with the relief of resignation and excess. Their lugubrious pleasure enticed her — one could almost imagine an alluring throng of squabbling, lost, aimless proto-souls from which humans took form and became complete, sovereign beings; lying perpetually in wait, they offered a tempting relapse into that primal formlessness. Most of those around her seemed to withstand such temptation without batting an eye and gave in to it with the greatest equanimity. That *might* have been because they were neither receptive nor convalescent enough to sense when their road began to slope downward, toward dissolution. Malin, meanwhile, reacted with every nerve, leaving her only one choice: to distance herself from all such distractions.

And there were other things to provide an antidote to the chaos, gathering, simplifying, fortifying. They belonged to the world of the sun. A house, a chair, a glass... strength and consolation could stream from every surface and line. They weren't 'beautiful' — they were beacons lighting the way toward the possibility of living. Malin understood what she never had before: how deeply serious and universally important *art* is.

Crisis

When Mother played the piano to herself in their large, empty parlor, Malin would often sneak in to listen. The same prayer always lay upon her lips: 'Let it be something by Bach!' No one belonged so surely to the sun and the cosmos as Bach. In fact she knew too little about music to fully understand what made him so ineffable. But behind the harmonic progressions, amid the relentless control of rhythm, cutting through its technical bravura and its 'difficulty,' she discerned a way of *relating*, that was undeniable.

She weighed the value of everything, every little thing within her reach, according to the same sensitive scales of all value, asking: will this lead to clarity or away from it, to equilibrium or away from it, to health or away from it? Put more simply and appropriately: to Siv or away from her.

She was on a voyage to discover Siv.

Thus, the spring opened wider still, and each new day approached with the prospect of excitement, the adventure of all adventures.

'Of course, it's beautiful — and yet I can't shake the urge to say: *tant de bruit pour une omelette!*'

Principal Melling had uttered the phrase in an irreverent comment about Kellgren's poem, 'New Creation.' She had attended one of Professor Fjell's lectures in literary history and was discussing it amicably with the professor, who, for his part, was terrified at its blasphemous implications.

Hearing the words in passing, Malin grew pensive. *Une omelette?*

But that's what it was. A piece of cake to some, to others, the burning bush. Either side would have difficulty convincing the other. Even if one side enlisted every word in a language the other could still say: but those are just words and that's all they'll ever be.

On the one side: *Who could depict that devouring light that shatters a soul into fragments and then fuses it back together into new life?*

On the other: *Who could take such pompous words seriously?*

Comical indeed, of course it was comical! Before, Malin would have been writhing, ridiculous and ashamed, like a snake in an anthill. But not now. Now, something more important outweighed the shame.

The stout, sullen little twenty-year-old Malin Forst must have looked comical plodding beside Siv Lindvall, faithfully, day after day, from southern campus to the Central Station in order to be in her presence as long as she could. And that timid, wide-eyed look of admiration she directed toward Siv's lovely profile — comical, just comical! Had she been a young man walking alongside the young woman he secretly idolized — maybe then, but just maybe, she could have been taken seriously. Had she been a young woman walking this same route with the man she secretly loved — that too would have verged on laughable, aroused disapproval even. But this situation — was, at the very least, irredeemably comical! If not worse.

Growing suddenly stiff and at a loss for words, being dull as a doornail, certainly doesn't make things less ridiculous. A void expands within you, and not the kind of calm, receptive emptiness that can be filled, but rather a brimming emptiness that leaves you lock-jawed. And it always happens just as you're on the brink of satisfying some longing you've had for a long time. It's easy when you're practicing on your own: 'There's something I'd like to tell you — I wanted to show you.' — But the instant your long-stifled desires glimpse a way out, panic ensues. Casting themselves over one another, blocking and shutting one another out, wrestling and constricting one another, they eventually run out of room to move. The forces of desire reach an impasse; from outside, it will look like death. No more thinking, no more feeling, your will: paralyzed.

You continue walking and walking without the strength to utter a sound. Only later, when you cross Riksbron bridge do you manage to blurt out a few words that stumble clumsily over one another:

'Look how early the willows are this year!'

They surely are, yes, their light green veils hang gently, spring-like above the glittering currents of Norrström, but the instant you utter the words they become as unimportant to you as the cobblestones under your feet and you aren't sure what you really wanted to say — but it definitely wasn't what came out. Everything you really long to express remains hidden in some corner of your being. Binding and guarding it with all of your inner effort drains everything else of its vibrancy, its life, its reality.

Afterwards, when you're by yourself again and the spasm eases up, you're utterly drained. Only then do you notice a pain in your foot. You pull off your shoe to find a thorn sticking straight up into your heel and realize it must have been there for a while because your shoe is full of blood. You've been in such a state of tension that you didn't even feel it!

You could offer some superficial explanation to the others, the ones with the omelet, precisely because it's so laughable. But they'd just shrug their shoulders and say 'Dear child, really, what are you fussing about?' — And how would you explain that you endure tongue-tied exhaustion and deathly humiliation and your own ridiculousness all the time, and this is relatively inconsequential, except in one case: if it is also apparent to Siv? And how could you make them understand that you wouldn't hesitate to subject yourself to that same humiliation again and again, at the slightest opportunity?

Of course, one understandable reason is that you constantly hope everything will change. So many things appear awful and insurmountable in the beginning, but then eventually change. Why not this too? Since we know nothing for certain about the future it appears enormous, extending indefinitely, formless, and full of surprises. You tread carefully, testing each step as you go, and don't anticipate anything beyond that day, but you don't despair about that either. Instead, you hope: for the ability to accomplish far more than we are able to desire.

But above all, something else impels you. Or more precisely, makes you choose this ridicule with your entire soul. How could they understand *that*?

It might seem obvious that a person's outer lines and movements cannot express one thing while being something else, deep inside. Neither is it surprising when this is ultimately confirmed. But it didn't occur to you that this new side of the same being could be so astounding and so exciting. It makes you industrious. You can no longer afford to miss a single second of it.

This is how it happened:

During the mid-morning break, a group of friends were engaged in a lively discussion. Who wouldn't want to be part of a lively discussion? True, Siv was there, and consequently also the law decreeing that Malin keep her distance. But

Crisis

wasn't that law on the verge of expiring? It had been written long ago, for someone who was ill.

Those who spoke were full of disdain and skepticism. They were lambasting modern art, currently Cubism.

'In no way shape or form can a person be a collection of boxes!' one said.

'At Christmas I saw a painting at an art exhibition where a man's face was *green*. I'm not exaggerating, it was *green!*' said another.

'Well of course,' a third explained, 'you have to do something to be considered original and if you can't come up with anything else then you make things square that are round in real life.'

But to that Siv slowly replied:

'I once heard a painter explain that Cubism isn't art for everyone, exactly, but rather an art for artists.'

Is it so strange that upon hearing such a statement your eyes fill with tears and you feel the urge to sing out loud or fall down and worship? Perhaps it is strange. But no, no, surely if the others could understand anything it would be that — they would have to be blind not to! —Of course, you neither sing out, nor fall prostrate to the ground. You stand motionless instead, allowing the impression to penetrate as deeply and imprint itself as permanently on your soul as possible. Later that night you know that you have won something new.

And what if they still don't understand? How could you make them see?

Or describe how unaffectedly she stood among the others? How their sarcasm had no effect on her, how she was not caught up in their laughter. She stood firmly with both feet planted firmly on the solid foundation of what she herself had experienced. That in itself sufficed. Or describe her refusal to pronounce any judgement before it had matured, a refusal undertaken with the slow deliberation of a somnambulist? It resembled the slowness of fruit ripening, of a seed ripening. How to describe how a person radiates with the knowledge that all things come to be through the strength of a good kernel? All seeds lie in wait for the steady hand that will put them to use. And those who haven't yet found their way to this good kernel, can only direct onward those who ask, in the direction of those who already know it. — Yes, try to describe the eyes and mouth and voice and shimmer and rhythm of one who dares show integrity in the face of existence — integrity enough only to trust the judgment of those with experience who have made discoveries.

This you know as well: approaching existence in earnest requires mastery of this ultimate integrity.

Oh, you have developed a notion of justice — but finally come to see it was nothing but a watery broth of negative haziness! Instead of an immense, generous grandeur.

A sculptor could probably describe it better, or a musician.

But would the others understand then either?

Even if Siv herself had been deeply involved in the discussion, if she had been a Cubist painter, her tone of voice would have remained just as calm. She would have had no cause either to attack or offend. Not because she feared she would violate some prohibition of antagonistic feelings or actions, but precisely because there was nothing she feared. In her state of calm certainty, the idea of being personally attacked or offended didn't even occur to her. Either others were in the know, or they weren't — and that was a matter that could be investigated. It was difficult to know in a case like this whether: *to Siv, the object superseded the human* — meaning: to her, reality itself was so captivating that humanity's vain claims to an illusory truth were merely ridiculous child's play — or whether it wouldn't be a better and a more fitting description to say the opposite: *to her the human superseded the object* — meaning: she had sworn no allegiance and was bound by no opinion; and thus everything remained available to her as an implement — the human superseded all objects to use each as it was intended, a purpose unto itself.

You have developed a notion of objectivity — but really, as it turns out it was nothing more than anxiety-laden, ascetic denial. Instead of power and freedom!

But when a few simple words can open the doors to an entirely new approach to things and reality, an entire holy

Crisis

attitude of observation and thought — how could anyone still care about their own ridiculousness or the torment of freezing up? Such concerns become fundamentally meaningless in the face of the thirst inside you that can only be quenched by the most noble of wines: Humanity.

Admittedly, this causes a great ruckus. The omelet in this case: Siv's words, which were quite natural and in actual fact not especially momentous ...

They say that love is blind, because it sees and appraises in its own way. But isn't it love — and only love — that truly sees?

Karin Boye

But then, there will be nights when you must survey your boundaries and move your fence posts to accommodate new and humiliating discoveries. And those nights will come, again and again.

The first was prompted by the simple and natural discovery of a simple and natural fact. There was a man Siv liked — which ought not to have been surprising in and of itself. Malin had hurried to walk with her after class, but when she came out, she saw Siv standing on the other side of the street speaking to a young man who had been waiting for her. The expression on Siv's face as it tilted upwards to speak with him was overwhelmingly beautiful.

Staggering more than walking, boarding the wrong train, ending up far away in Handen instead of Tullinge, and arriving home several hours late, Malin remained absolutely indifferent to it all, even Father's comments. The whole thing was laughable, if somehow expected. And yet, *that* was precisely what she had expected least of all! The last thing she believed possible.

She should have known better — she told herself, lying awake and staring out into the darkness — no one can possess what is highest and most beautiful, no one can lay claim to that. It's fleeting, like a revelation. The most you can hope for is to see and grasp it and then attempt to grow into its likeness. What is highest and most beautiful evades capture, even in human form.

She must survey her boundaries and grow beyond them, transcend them.

Crisis

The persistent difficulty of bringing that about was most perceptible in the pain she felt now. She hadn't realized just how narrow-minded and primitively greedy she had been. Only now could she see that she had embarked upon the false path of mistaking a person for what is highest and most beautiful.

It's so dangerous to leave behind those safe, impersonal places where you still take pleasure in a human being as if enjoying a flower, and allow yourself to be lured into what is altogether too personal, toward what we call a soul. It's so strange that this, the soul, could be the entryway to unknown, all-too human, intensely private, obscure desires ...

This was clearly something she would have to annihilate in order to surmount it. One has to find a way past what is intensely personal and singular, to find how to grasp the most exquisite beauty as entirely impersonal, even if it happens to reveal itself in the figure of a person. Clearly, she had overestimated her own strength, overestimated herself in every way. She had failed to account for her all-too-human insignificance, had not yet come to terms with it.

Easier said than done! What good are wisdom, principles or rules in the face of a human being! She knew only one thing: she was in pain.

The agony intensified, and Siv was there. Close to her, surrounding her. She felt only searing flames — and Siv. Searing flames, Siv, and agony.

Why deny that it hurt, when there was no way around the pain. Why numb yourself with lofty words about what is high and beautiful, when that wasn't everything. And it wasn't! The whole thing was still Siv.

It couldn't be so, it wasn't so! She had to stop caring about all that was personal, degrading... Had to throw it to the ground, pulverize it. Had to rise out of this low humanity to reach the fresh, cool heights of the unsullied and impersonal. Fight! She had to fight, had to, had to...!

But Siv remained. Not just as flames and agony, but also in the intensity of her calm, clear simplicity. In the light of this calm, clear simplicity Malin felt ashamed of her flailing about, as she once had in gymnastics class.

The prevailing demands all around us are but hollow, titanic theater. Longing remains the heart of our being, guiding us to mature.

All you can do is strip yourself of false, inhuman claims and relinquish your constructions — how many times is that now? — knowing you remain vulnerable within the longing that caused so much pain in your being. This you do without heroic gesture.

Because I have seen you, Siv.

Crisis

All those heavy black books! They looked so hostile amid the fair little mites. Why is every holy book black? Surely it's no coincidence.

The first-graders sat piously, their hands folded upon their tiny desks an indication of the fact that it wasn't everyday knowledge that they were there to absorb, but profound truths about life and lofty things. Small hands that would all too readily venture out on their own, that yearned to draw stick figures on desktops or inside the covers of textbooks (each equally reprehensible), or fiddle with their pens and build towers on top of the inkwell with erasers or a teetering pile of books stacked one on top of the other. It was never a good thing when those little hands got loose, if they happened to, but during scripture lessons it was entirely out of the question. During that class, hands remained fixed upon the desk in front of them — those dumb, unruly little hands.

Malin suddenly remembered a directive from her childhood: 'Paws off! Look but don't touch!' — not exactly applicable to this situation.

She sat at the back of the room with the other students from the college, notebooks in hand, to observe Fröken Zender where she sat in the corner. The head of the Christianity curriculum for the first grade, Fröken Zender was a tall, pale woman with an unassuming and kindly yet determined demeanor.

Fröken Zender's pedagogy was brilliant. Her previous lesson had been an introduction, equally elegant and skillful, to the rewarding topic of the shepherd and his flock. She began by drawing upon the children's own experience with sheep and lambs — which though admittedly not extensive, could still be employed more thoroughly and concretely. She subsequently taught them about the shepherd and his care, conjuring up idyllic scenes of him and his flock before relating these images more broadly to human life. 'And we, too, have a good shepherd to lead us... now who could that be, children?' — That, they had no problem understanding. She then drew a distinction between an earthly shepherd and a heavenly one: no human shepherd could match the attention, strength, patience, or foresight of a heavenly one, whose benevolence and power were both eternal and limitless. And then, finally, Fröken Zender read the first verses of the psalm they would eventually discuss and made the children recite in chorus: 'The Lord is my shepherd; I shall not want. He maketh me to lie down in green pastures: he leadeth me beside the still waters. He restoreth my soul...'

Malin had been watching little Magnus Anderson. From behind, at least, his mop of ash blond hair looked as pious as all the others did. But what sense did he make of, 'I shall not want'? Did he imagine it to be a dream that would be fulfilled in the future, or something else? It had been a model lesson in the most literal sense of the word: it had remained entirely at the children's level and impeccably concrete. But in order for this 'I shall not want' to be applicable in any way to Magnus Anderson it would have to be expanded and made considerably more abstract — far beyond the horizons of a first-grader. The thought of his bare legs in the rain! His stunted being! He was likely not the only one either. The students at the grade school generally came from well-off working-class homes, but there were always exceptions — and there are always prosperous homes, for that matter, where things aren't as they should be, where children are weighed down by burdens altogether too heavy for them to bear. She couldn't know for sure — but at the very least, saying that Magnus Anderson wanted for nothing was an exaggeration — that much was certain.

'You'll probably say I'm fussy or nitpicking,' she said to Nanni Fransson as they were walking out, 'and I know that it was a good lesson — but it all makes me so *angry*. If they

Crisis

mean that less fortunate children, and I know of at least one here who is having a particularly rough time at home, should feel grateful *no matter what*, simply because they belong to a Christian congregation that allows them access to holy truths and all of that, then they should come out and say it, instead of ignoring it and pretending that those children don't have anything to complain about ... Perhaps I'm not making myself clear ... Because it's just *wrong* ... In school, we had to sing a song about a cake-shop owner that actually ended with the words: 'If you can pay, you can stay, but if you can't, you shan't!' That's at least honest and true, if you think about it. No one could deny it. But the school denied it! Ordering the world in such a way would be immoral; hence they didn't. Instead, they made us sing: 'If you're sweet, come get a treat. If you misbehave, then none today!'

'It certainly is false,' said Nanni Fransson merrily, 'and immoral in *the worst sense of the word!* Just wait, we'll soon come to the part about miseries too, and that they're easily overcome. I figured it out. Ellen Eriksson will have to teach The Shadow of the Valley of Death, oh boy, The Shadow of the Valley of Death! That means you'll get: "Thou anointest my head with oil; my cup runneth over." Aren't you happy about that?'

'It probably won't be so bad. At least with that verse you can talk about inviting people to parties the whole time. I wouldn't trade places with Ellen Eriksson for anything.'

'Hmm, then I'll be the one who has to check that they've grasped the main idea: "Surely goodness and mercy shall follow me all the days of my life, etcetera." And then Karin Fägersten will have to start something new.'

'But it makes me so angry, I just can't help it. What good can it possibly do to pretend like that?'

'I don't know! Maybe it's easier? You can't very well tell children how things really are. They're scared enough as it is, the poor things.'

Malin fell silent. Magnus Anderson didn't need anyone to tell him how things really were, he knew. But what she wouldn't give to see the world through his eyes, even for a

Karin Boye

few minutes, to see whether the world he experienced and the pastoral world of the shepherd merged or remained separate in his mind.

The following lesson was Märta Balke's. It was no easy task to follow in Fröken Zender's footsteps, but she walked boldly onto the path that had already been blazed. The children easily understood that sheep experienced danger as well. The creativity with which they imagined everything that could befall a little lamb nearly became too much for Märta Balcke and she sat there peering nervously at her exceedingly detailed lesson plan. But she pressed on to the story of a sick little lamb who was having a dull time in its pen but then, suddenly heard a voice, the voice of the shepherd, and the little lamb felt such joy — or as it's also called, *restoration* — just like when you're sick and your mother sits at the edge of your bed and makes everything better, even though you're sick. (The line about the sick lamb was an excellent illustration artfully devised by Märta Balcke. The children all understood it as it referred to an earlier part of her text: 'He restoreth my soul.') The children then readily offered examples of how their mothers fussed over them when they felt sick. Some even read them stories.

('Exactly right, you could say that your mother restores you,' Märta concurred attentively.)

Then she returned to the idea of dangers along the road, drawing a parallel to human life. We too can get lost. We too can fall down dangerous ravines that are difficult to climb out of. Now, can anyone tell me what you think the dangers along the road might be?

'Like when we go the wrong way in the woods,' a boy well-versed in fairy tales suggested.

'Yes, but that's not the worst way to get lost. We could get lost in a different way, anywhere, at home, or even in school.'

'Like when we don't do as we're told?' another one guessed. (Such symbolism was not entirely unfamiliar to them.)

'Yes, that's right.'

At that, the students obliged Märta with a shower of examples of disobedience and above all of how categorically obedient they themselves were. Only one little fellow confessed, to his visible satisfaction, that he didn't always brush his teeth, even though his mother told him to.

Malin's glances once again found the back of Magnus Anderson's neck. He was probably fairly obedient. He went out begging, after all, when his parents told him to. Or had he offered resistance? If he had, it was probably long forgotten by this point. 'Children are like little Pharisees,' Fröken Zender had said once during a methodology lesson.

She sat there, on tenterhooks. A storm was gathering within her. Her thoughts began racing at a feverish pace, as they inevitably did when something agitated her. 'The objective is to lay the foundations of the child's first religious and ethical conceptions,' she read quietly to herself from the education plan. Last time it was religion: the pastoral world of the shepherd. This time it was the ethical: obedience. Everyone should be obedient and well-behaved. It was the most fundamental command. One so holy that it had to be taught with hands clasped together. It's easier that way. Dear God, dear God, to the extent that you exist, how much you must hate your preachers who exploit you as both punishment and its sweet reward ... And the one who they crucified as a miscreant in Golgatha, was he truly *obedient and nice* ... I don't know if he was, anyhow, he is now, and obedient unto death too, yes, until his crucifixion... And that was the main point...?

The command to love: they wouldn't learn that, the highest of all ethical principles, until more advanced grades. Thou shalt love! Thou shalt! In other words: love bears all things, believes all things, hopes all things, suffers long and is kind, is not provoked, does not parade itself, does not behave rudely, does not envy, does not seek its own ... These rules are for you and me, Magnus. It's easier that way. How would we behave otherwise? Presumably in the most troublesome way. When we grow old enough to have our own children or disciples or subordinates, then perhaps we'll be glad that they too were taught about clasped hands and solemn, threatening black books lying on the pulpit. Better that than some standard set

Karin Boye

of rules that can be criticized or changed from one day to the next.

Just one thing, though: what in the name of everything that has been despised and trampled down by reason does this have to do with being moral? It should be called: The Doctrine of the Authority's Prohibition Against Revolt. But morality is something else ...

It's something beautiful. It's something bright and liberating. It's something you don't need to be commanded to love. I know what it is — — —

She bent over her notebook and wrote:

'Is the cornerstone of an ethical life really *to be obedient and well-behaved*?'

Nanni Fransson read it, and after contemplating a moment, wrote her reply:

'Anything else would be beyond a first-grader.'

Malin: 'Then we could wait a while to teach them ethics.'

Nanni: 'But then, I wonder: doesn't obedience still have to be the basis for all ethics, even if it's at a higher level?'

Malin couldn't think of an answer. On one hand, it probably was true, in a way — to love and worship something was also to obey it — but on the other hand, she had a strong feeling that there was a difference between the two. She made a hesitant gesture signaling her uncertainty as Märta Balcke read aloud to the class in a clear, distinct voice:

'... He leadeth me in the paths of righteousness for His name's sake.'

Four heads in the back bowed down over their notebooks; four hands scribbled: 'She didn't explain: *for His name's sake.*'

Later, when they analyzed Märta's lesson together, Malin couldn't help commenting:

'Our Christianity lessons always make it sound as if obedience is the highest and only virtue.'

A vague smile of understanding spread across Fröken Zender's face. Fröken Forst certainly sounded headstrong at times, but perhaps it was only nervousness.

'Well,' she said, 'in a sense that's natural in that each age group must be given what they need. Otherwise, you could

Crisis

be correct, Fröken Forst, that a little variety can be a good thing. Lying, for example, is something children are of course very familiar with, even if they adamantly deny that they themselves do it. The same goes for being unkind. Or sulky. Or mean to their friends, or to animals. You're quite right that we could flesh out the same lesson a bit.'

But to Malin, the entire world seemed to echo with the battle raging between the Power and the Rebellion. This was Lucifer's struggle — Lucifer the Bringer of Light, called by his enemies, the Evil One. Outside, the air was thick with the combatants' roar. People bustled through crowded streets in the service of one side or the other, sometimes without even knowing which. Messengers from one side or the other hid behind hardened human masks. Here too, in corridors and classrooms, armies of light pursued their dark enemies, impressing the holy mark of shame and guilt into their faces when they fell. Still with this brand on their forehead, they rose yet again, ugly with bad conscience, their gaze timid, their backs stooped. Even lacking the sanctioned confidence of the luminous ones, the disobedient and rebellious rose up, in the struggle for something so precious that neither shame nor guilt could frighten them into submission. Led by Lucifer — The Bringer of Light, known by the enemy as the Evil One.

When Magnus Anderson and Malin met on the stairs a few days later she beamed with the tender feeling of a secret camaraderie. He was no longer the prosecutor who demanded that she be willing to suffer. He was another little, battle-worn soldier. She would fight for him as if her own life were at stake.

My people!

Karin Boye

Morning prayers are dreadful. As if rearing their heads to demand new sustenance, the familiar words and sensations summon up everything that Malin seeks to leave behind. Here she stands, face to face with her old conscience, as a sinner — yet with a new conscience as well. It's a matter of not letting up, a matter of knowing which side to stand on. Had she been given the choice she would have gladly avoided morning prayers and everything they represented. Naturally, that was impossible. So here she'll sit, well-behaved, always keeping an eye on her former judge, in order to expose him, to convince him, to drown out his voice.

Briskly and resolutely, Principal Melling steps up to the lectern. Two days earlier she had heard news from the continent; the mournful reports of attempts to alleviate post-war destruction had shaken her. Her strong, practical impulse to help found no outlet, however, and was condemned to wither away in impotence. Today she would address the topic of suffering in the world instead.

... scarcely three years have passed since the bloodshed of this world war ended yet we've already calmly resigned ourselves to forgetting it...

MALIN 2. Yes, forget, let us forget! In order to continue living we must forget. Grant us our lovely idylls, grant us consolation and respite! Allow us to forget ourselves in life rather than remember ourselves to death.

MALIN 1. That you could be so selfish!

MALIN 2. Gladly! Gladly! Why shouldn't I be selfish? Any good reason not to? Or simply because 'selfishness' is an ugly word?

Crisis

... while large parts of the world remain burdened with horrible suffering ...

MALIN 2. We know this already. It's something we can ascertain objectively: two times two is four. Is there anything I can do to help? No? Okay then, we might as well go enjoy a cup of coffee in the meanwhile.

MALIN 1. Enjoying yourself as your brothers and sisters suffer ...

MALIN 2. Help so that you pull yourself under as well, you mean? Admit it. You're nothing but an idiot. I refuse to allow an idiot like you to control me. Hold your tongue along with all of its ugly, alluring insults! Who knows — there may come a time when I can actually help and maybe I will. But it won't be because I should or ought to, but rather because I — want to!

... if we've been spared, it's not so that we can continue, like cowards, to avoid the responsibility of bearing our fair share ...

MALIN 2. Ah, now this I recognize. 'Suffer!' everyone says, followed by, 'For He has suffered!' And you say it in hushed voices as if out of deference to something magnificent. You're all competing to be the one who suffers most, like little boys bragging about their favorite sportsman. You despise health and joy as banal, unless, of course, they've come at the great cost of that glorious, deep suffering! Can't you see the extent of your blasphemy? — Oh, health! Oh, beautiful, quiet, natural health, what a rarity you are, what a goal to aim for. You alone are worthy of worship! Siv! Save us!

MALIN 1. Even a non-Christian can see that the Principal is right. We must act as human beings, it's that simple. We can't deny our responsibility to, or solidarity with those less fortunate. Far be it from us to dance to jazz by their well of anguish. To withdraw from our experience of suffering in the world is to stand on the side of the executioner. Either victim or executioner, there is no third option in this world!

MALIN 2. If I fight, I fight to win, not to fall. To all of you, my people, my fellow soldiers, I say: should I fall, continue as if it were an accident — not the culmination of what my life means. Say that our suffering is merely one of life's missteps.

Karin Boye

Don't ask how we suffered, that's immaterial, and even shameful. Ask instead what we accomplished in health, in joy, in victory! That is our honor and our gift that will endure.

... let us pray that our hearts don't grow hard. Let them remain open to the lamentations that disturb our blithe peace of mind ...

MALIN 2. Let's us pray that our hearts harden into joyful crystals ...

MALIN 1. Do you sincerely believe that you can harden yourself against me for any length of time, against me, your conscience?

MALIN 2. You can go by any name you wish, I don't care. You're a mollusk that will be poisoned by reason, by clear, pure, godly reason, reason that no amount of terror can alter — reason that provides a stronghold against fear! I'll starve you out! I certainly won't be attending morning prayers all my life.

... for thine is the kingdom ...

MALIN 2. It wafts through the ages like a cool breeze imbued with the power to build, assemble: the dream of Hellas. Nothing more than a mirage. But in its glorious, cool springs, flagellants wash the blood from their backs. The dream of a pagan Hellas of light, that never existed in reality. The dream of a goal. — Siv! Refuge!

WHITE. You've burst through your enclosure and claimed new space. The game is shifting to your advantage. And yet I laugh, and laugh, and laugh. A moment ago we stood at the threshold of birth, you and I, and you charged yourself with a combustive internal force, but I grasped at the external world and I nearly blocked you in! Now we stand here, at the door to a new, outer world — a larger community, of the masses. Do you wish to conquer that one too, you with your insatiable hunger!? Be assured, I will grasp again at this new outside, I seek anew the voice of Judgement! Listen! It's all around us, and it vanquishes everything. In a moment of weakness, as your guards lie sleeping, metal will once again awaken metal and block your path.

BLACK. She is metal herself! Sword and will, through and through!

WHITE. You will consume yourself in your own ravenous hunger.

BLACK. I'm still strong! And I live! — I will defy you.

WHITE. Let the game continue. *Garde la reine!*

Dialogue III: On Malin Forst

Crisis

THE CACTUS GROWER. I, for one, find it a bit touching to see the way that life, even in its most impoverished and stunted form, clings tightly to existence by any means possible. Isn't there something downright brave about that tenacity — that is, if we can talk about life force in terms of tenacity — perhaps it's somehow irregular to do so. It reminds me of those tiny gray cottages you see clinging to the inhospitable, barren mountainsides of the North — they're outposts of human life, at the very least, regardless of what that life may be.

THE AESTHETE. What do you mean, the most impoverished and stunted forms? Are you actually implying that it makes sense to refer to 'the most impoverished and stunted forms' in a case like this? Do you mean to say that the hypersensitivity of her soul, propelling her to the verge of ruin, toward the experience of Judgement Day, to places where people with thicker skins wouldn't dream of venturing, actually impoverishes her life? Isn't it instead a sublime drama worthy of deep reverence? Regardless of the facts on which it is based, isn't this ultimately the most profound form of conflict that nourishes all great art and elevates human life to tragedy? It's not something that can simply be wished out of existence. Can you conceive of a more tedious notion than that of idyllic eternal paradise? There's no need to fear it. This conflict will never die, and consequently neither will art. Human life will never be deprived of art's great, uplifting significance.

THE FUNCTIONALIST. To my mind, that's a heartless account of the suffering endured by a fellow human being struggling for her health. Using aesthetic criteria to assess such serious matters is indefensible. If neither health nor happiness can exist within your criteria, then perhaps your criteria need to be adjusted rather than your casting suspicion on health and happiness so as to take pleasure in the conflict as a 'sublime drama!' This is how I see the matter: we can probably all agree that, despite everything, this young person, Malin, now has a significantly more rational, and consequently more sound, approach to existence?

THE PRAGMATIST. Hmmm. Any approach could be called 'rational,' provided that it helps us live our lives. (I understand that you'll disagree with my definition of the term, but this is at least what I take 'rational' to mean.) Let's not forget that this isn't the first time Malin Forst has been prepared to embrace life. After her so-called conversion, she made the same claim, and who can say whether she wasn't even more prepared to fulfill it then than she is now? She's undergone a transformation — that's the most we can say of it. It's possible that it won't be the last one either. It's possible that this new approach to life which appears so liberating will eventually seem as binding and repressive as the old one does to her now.

WOMAN WITH COMMON SENSE. Exactly! I agree, Malin Forst has quite simply undergone a transformation, and a rather sad one. 'More sound!' you call it, but you can't mean that seriously! She has always had the predisposition of an inwardly religious, rather highly-strung but undeniably morally elevated young girl. She feels a strong affinity with all humans and, therefore, a great personal responsibility. In other words: she's a *very* healthy person, if you only look below the surface. But then she fell ill. I understand that some might say that her illness was related to her previous outlook on life, but I don't believe that. She was well and then she fell ill, it's as simple as that. No need for any far-fetched explanation; this kind of thing happens all the time. She is, and continues to be, sick. Because the egoism she's developing, even turning it into a kind of program, in my opinion, is much less healthy than any torment she might have previously experienced on account of the evil in the world. In my opinion, it's altogether healthier, fitting even, to be tormented by such things. And as for falling in love, that episode strikes me as absolutely disgusting. I myself am so thoroughly healthy that I feel almost physically repelled by it.

A SCHOOLMISTRESS. From my perspective, her falling in love is the most idealistic and pure thing imaginable precisely *because* it has so little to do with physical bodies! If you mistake *that* experience for being physical, then you really do have a perverted imagination! Such schoolgirl crushes are so common that you could almost call them normal, and I can guarantee, speaking as someone who's seen a lot of this sort of thing in my days, that they don't have anything at all to do with physical bodies. Of course, twenty is a bit old to be having these sorts of feelings, but some people are late developers when it comes to feelings. Having met Malin Forst in person, I can tell you there's something so pure in her eyes, pure enough to counter any base, physical thought that even approaches smutty fantasies. — Regarding the question of her egoism and her other highly-strung views, young people today don't actually mean most of what they declare so programmatically. — When it comes down to it: I don't think Malin Forst will necessarily turn out to be a bad person.

ACADEMIC INSTRUCTOR IN ETHICS. Naturally, it's still *possible* that she'll become an unimpeachable citizen. But having abandoned religion and her conscience to pursue some indefinite and indefinable 'desire,' she's no longer on stable ground, which means that at the very least there's the likelihood that she'll veer off track somehow or other, perhaps also in some outwardly evident way as a member of civic society. You couldn't hope for a clearer demonstration than this case that human beings today no longer possess a moral authority — free from the doubt that generates reflection — to grip and guide their inner life. Had she never begun to suspect that the demands exacted by the laws of morality were unreasonable, this entire neurosis-generating conflict would never have arisen. In this instance, the moral force was too weak. — I'll repeat what I've always said: *a person's deepest mental wellbeing is better served by going under, intellectually speaking, than by being 'cured' of her sense of sin in any other way than by remorse and forgiveness.*

Karin Boye

PASTOR. Let me just add that it was a mistake for her to go to that well-intentioned but somewhat hazy Fröken Mogren. If only Malin Forst had followed her initial impulse to look up her confirmation teacher or some other experienced spiritual advisor he surely would have talked sense into her and helped change the direction of her thinking. Her religiosity was perhaps something of a danger sign from the outset — wasn't it a bit too influenced by quietism? A bit too much of the eternal mysteries? Naturally, that kind of thing eventually just makes the will weak.

DOCTOR. As far as trying to 'talk sense into her' goes, that accomplished hardly anything in a case like Malin Forst. I doubt very much that dogmatic heresy could be blamed for her symptoms! In fact, I'm rather afraid that had she grown up in other circumstances and with other ideals it wouldn't have made the least bit of difference. The girl, simply put, was pretty clearly degenerate. That much was evident just from her ecstatic, not to say hysterical, tendencies. In all likelihood, she was predestined to suffer from melancholia — such fears of damnation are of course, so typical — and nothing will change that. Her opinions and attitudes toward life or whatever you want to call them, might shift, but her nature will stay the same. In actual fact, that Doctor Ringström *was* a fairly wise man, despite being a social butterfly. There was just not much else to be done, I can tell you that!

TRAINING COLLEGE PRINCIPAL. If everything were actually as simple and hopeless as you say it is, then we would be best to scrap the heavy taxes funding our education system, and just let our children's inherited characteristics develop on their own, without any interference. I have to say, I think the college that Malin Forst attended was rather peculiar. At our college, we simply don't have the time to get absorbed in ourselves — or as the doctor puts it so prettily: in our 'melancholy' — in that unhealthy way. And I am absolutely certain that had we discovered any such tendencies toward anything like that we surely would have found a way to counteract them. I agree entirely with Malin Forst's father on that point: this is not a matter for doctors, but rather a question of education.

Crisis

Her story teaches us that much. Doesn't she eventually change precisely because she takes responsibility for her own education? It's merely a coincidence that this coincides with a crush. It might just as well have happened in a more common and natural way — namely in connection with some religious conversion or encounter with some great personality — in other words, without all of the romantic rubbish. It's still basically the same thing, that is, the encounter with a higher moral reality. The fact that Malin Forst's crisis is leading her away from Christianity is unfortunate, but it might very well be a necessary stage in her own development. I suspect she'll return to it when she's older and more sensible.

MAN WITH A WEDDING RING. 'Higher ethical reality!?' Are you really so convinced that the image that Malin Forst referred to as 'Siv' corresponded to reality at all? The whole thing was a gigantic illusion, I'm afraid. Many young men also have similar notions about the one their heart adores only to be cruelly disillusioned when they happen to be successful in their pursuit. Personally, I'd call that 'higher ethical reality' precisely what it is: a beautiful mask donned by our urges to deceive us. The truth is simply not as alluring.

GENTLE PERSON. If that's the case then you haven't been seeking the truth with the same loving trust with which you sought the illusion. When I see a beautiful veil torn to shreds before my eyes I always think: any reality that could weave and employ such a veil must be superior. And when I glimpsed behind the veil, I never found what I was looking for — not ever — but as long as I accepted that, I found other things, things that resounded more deeply and with a sweeter ripeness than I could ever imagine existed. And that's why, from my point of view, I prefer to agree with what seems to be Malin Forst's point: that we must entrust ourselves to our desire. We discover nothing through fear and antagonism, no matter what path we take. Only with love do we find everything, along every single path.

Which one is it? Is it blurry? Is that a sufficient explanation? No, I know it isn't. But at least I've learned one thing from this

Karin Boye

story as I have from others like it: you should never be too sure about what you don't know.

As usual, the graduation ceremony was held in the large assembly hall.

The entire population of students at the college, swollen, augmented by parents and guardians, poured en masse into the space enclosed by the tall, white walls. The soles of their shoes scraped and shuffled absent-mindedly across the floor as the ranks slowly crammed themselves into the rows of benches. Through the wide, tall windows the blue summer light streamed in, intense and calming. And inside, the butterfly wings of brightly colored ribbons tied in bows flexed themselves gently in a surreptitious sign that they would soon heed the call to freedom that awaited outside. Even those who had never felt unduly burdened by their time at school awoke that day with the impression of a homeland awaiting them, somewhere on a vast plain, a place they had forgotten, where their desires would be fulfilled. Muscles and ligaments stretched and creaked, like yawning cats. The sweet premonition of a delectable lawlessness filled them.

'Into the sheep pen for the last time!' someone whispered irreverently behind Malin as she and her entire graduating class jostled in through the doors, all dressed in white. Another answered just as merrily:

'This pen, at least!'

Those graduating sat at the front, facing their teachers who were ranged in high-backed chairs along the front of the stage decorated with greenery. Opposite Malin sat Professor Fjell. She was a kind person and had often been kind to Malin, sometimes positively maternal. Even so, it was hardly painful to say goodbye to her or any of the others. They were all part of a big, uniform mass that no longer required any kind of farewell. Malin's departure had already taken place. She had already torn herself loose. She was already outside.

Fjell was wearing the same watch chain with which she had toyed in such nervous fervor on the day of the final examination. Had she really been that anxious? But why? Maybe it was an attempt to use suggestion to instill students with the same expectant feeling of import that they would have felt taking their college entrance exams, underlining the solemnity of the occasion. As far as Malin was concerned, it hadn't worked. The events surrounding her exam had felt like acts in a play. Naturally she had played her part, and it was not by any means dull, but she had not been able to summon up any great sense of gravity in the moment or for her results. No matter, it was all fine. — She had already been outside, even then.

Yes, she was outside, solitarily, serenely beyond it all. All representation and signification had slipped away and now appeared tiny and distant. The ornamentation on the sunlit walls no longer tempted her to contemplation. Compared to the ray of sunlight itself, which was warm and bright, it seemed ephemeral, no longer real. Oh, that stream of sunlight — that was more real than all of the solemnity put together. It was nothing more than what it was, and signified nothing beyond that. It was primal and undeniable — a gift that couldn't be questioned. Whereas a celebration like this one ... It reminded her of the feeling she had as a child sitting at a grand, formal dinner punctuated by long speeches: why did they do that? It was a world foreign to her now. The world of representation. Then again, here she sat herself, bearing the name Malin Forst, a person both clear and recognizable, just as clear and recognizable as the person who sat here six months ago. There wasn't even any trickery about it. No bridge connected the world of reality with that of illusion. There was no reason to resist everything that was illusion. It was just that that other world cut right through the gossamer, the heavy, transforming world that cared nothing for any superficial flourish, nor would it ever.

Crisis

A thought flickered through her mind that this wouldn't be the last time she would find herself within a large group of people while remaining outside it. She would pass through various circles and coteries in different company, be called: Malin Forst — oh, she's so and so and so — but deep down, behind the name and the smile and the accommodating demeanor she would remain in her own anonymity, secure, as if behind a wall. She would throw herself into festivities to her heart's content, all the while knowing: that not one of all these so-called friends could endure looking my reality in the eye — any more than I could endure theirs. Once you realize that, you can abandon everything, cut straight through all the illusion, be distinct from your name and simply sit in the sun, dipping your hand in the water, and be happy that you exist with no anxiety. You endure. In naked existence. Where none is young or old, wise or stupid, where there is neither good nor evil. Beyond everything we are equal in the onerous struggle for cosmos.

The more advanced classes from the grade school stood up to sing. Among them was the class she had taught, her class! Hers, because last term she had worked with them for a six-hour series of lessons and had grown so attached to them all that she had been both sad and moved when it was over. She could predict how each and every one of them would answer a question. Inga Person, with one silver-grey lock of hair, answered as she thought she was supposed to, foolish thing. Some meaning lay behind everything that shy Anna Lindstedt uttered, no matter how strange it sounded. And then there was Karin Andersson, who was both impulsive and a fantasist — — — A hot flush rose in Malin's cheeks as she recalled her lessons. The counter-reformation, it must have been, yes. She had taught them that: we Protestants, of course, don't believe that Catholics are damned ... This was the kind of intellectual problem she had had the cheek to allow them to inherit, in this world, in this world ... And though it was doubtful that this was the worst that had befallen them, she still felt a sudden desire to run up to them and shout: 'Everything's completely different now! I don't know any of that anymore! I'm with you

Karin Boye

now! I'm one of you!' — But they wouldn't understand, they were set to go forth into the hands of others who still knew. Others who weren't with them and who wanted to let them inherit all of that and much worse things as well. A shout resounded within her, with a stinging certainty:

My people!

To be outside isn't to be apart from your people, no, not from your people. No, it's to be closer to them than ever before.

Finally, the graduating class took the stage to sing their well-rehearsed songs for the last time. The last time! There, ahead of her, singing the second part, stood Siv, for the last time. After this day, Malin knew, they would rarely see each other.

But it wasn't a farewell either. For how can you lose something that's growing within you, like a tree? How could you even imagine that a graduation ceremony, or distance, or time, could ever obscure the utter fact, the very creation that was Siv? Such things were of no significance.

There she stood, willowy, upright, and dignified, with the radiant shimmer of gold and fruit in her skin, radiating with the good fortune of nature's happy nobility that sometimes falls upon a human being entirely unnoticed, like dew falling upon the grass. She stood there, her exterior and interior in perfect balance, mature in her own foundation, not the least lost. A human, wholly content, filled with a kind of vegetative wisdom, swaying on the narrow footbridge suspended over chaos.

The song hovered between playfulness and veneration:

> 'Oh, overgrown grove, oh filtering forest,
> Oh, meadow in darling spring!
> Sweet is the roses' voice, I surely sense it,
> And I know what the lilies' laughter brings.'

And Malin's neck straightened, she sang along almost inaudibly, as if in a secret confession of faith, the only faith she still possessed — and although it had neither shape nor knowledge, it professed a proud love beyond all reason, for life's eternal, obstinate will to live.

> 'For every winter has spring, and every autumn a hope,
> and tomorrow, all midnight is vanishing.
> I yearn for a sun and the voice of the roses,
> and for the meadows' darling spring.'

Translator's Afterword

Literary translation, not unlike Boye's literary production, can be a personal, creative endeavor with political implications. Translating and publishing this novel marks a concerted attempt to broaden a canon of modernist literature still dominated by white, straight, male Anglophone writers. But as a translator working in the academy, I am equally excited about the ways that translating a book like *Crisis* might open up the possibility for new forms of literary scholarship that draw no significant distinction between emotion and intellect, or between translation and the scholarly practice of literary criticism. This is a decidedly political proposition. *Crisis* is a book that screams out for the personal to be acknowledged and attended to rather than ignored or subdued in the name of objectivity or equivalence, and I have tried to hear that.

This novel, with all of its elegance and awkward peculiarities, has compelled me for half of my life — unlike any other book I've encountered. I was an awkward nineteen-year-old when I first read it in a course on Swedish women's literature at the University of Washington — an initial exposure that coincided with my first taste of Nietzsche, Freud, and Marx, all of whom Boye had engaged with to write it. Undaunted by the fact that Boye's prose would stretch my undergraduate Swedish skills to their utmost limits, I set out (pencil to paper, with a heavy, bound dictionary) to bring it into English. It was an automatic reflex. I was self-aware enough to know that it was a naïve undertaking, but I was convinced that being so close in age to Malin would afford me insight into her experience that would compensate for my deficiencies. Thinking back, I would like to believe that my

Amanda Doxtater

decision to translate *Crisis* went something like the moment when Malin first glimpses Siv sitting in front of her and is both struck and soothed by the beauty of her gently-sloping shoulders. As it did with Malin, the vision of Siv also offered me a reprieve of sorts after having made my way through a significant portion of a book that I still find largely perplexing (if wondrous). The scene sparked desire, and translation was the most appropriate way for me to express it. If undertaking the labor of translation began with a flush of infatuation, it eventually transformed into a project of admiration and even a kind of love. *Crisis* became the center of my own intellectual *Bildungsroman*. I returned to it as an MA student and wrote my thesis on the novel, comparing Malin to Diva, the protagonist in Monika Fagerholm's postmodern novel by the same name. The two protagonists had too many compelling similarities, I argued, to allow us to draw a sharp distinction between modernism and postmodernism. During this period, I had the fortunate opportunity to workshop a section of my draft in a translation seminar with the amazing translator, Tiina Nunnally. I finished my thesis, but set the translation aside for more than a decade.

When I took it up again, I was in my thirties, much closer to the age that Boye was when she wrote the book, allowing other layers of complexity in *Crisis* to reveal themselves to me. Differentiating the novel's proliferation of registers and voices now involved channeling Boye at age thirty-four as well as Malin at age twenty, a fascinating undertaking. As Margit Abenius suggests in her introduction to the 1953 edition of *Crisis* (reprinted in the 1955 edition), at age twenty, Boye understood that she was experiencing a crisis, but she remained largely ignorant of what that entailed. It wasn't until she could look back on that time in her life, equipped with new psychoanalytic tools and more life experience, that she could make sense of it. Translating took on new interest to me as a task that resonated more closely with Boye's artful reconstruction of herself as an unwitting twenty-year-old, allowing me to savor this dramatic irony even as I struggled

Translator's Afterword

to hold the novel's different voices and temporalities in my own mind at once.

As this iteration of *Crisis* is set to be published, I have now lived a longer life than Boye did. I grew into an academic with this book, and I also grew into a translator with it. In something approximating a full circle, I now work as a professor of Swedish Studies at the same institution where I first encountered the novel as a student. Even after so many years, I still identify with the experience of falling for someone who doesn't love you back, with all the disappointment and heartbreak that this entails. And I am perhaps more familiar with how the experience of intense physical desire can be heightened by thinking about it, analyzing it. Turning Siv into a 'principle' to reflect on, as Boye does, making her disappointment meaningful and beautiful and textual, accomplishes a brilliant rationalization of disappointment. While this might have been a cynical move, what makes *Crisis* so endearing is that Malin's fate, as well as Boye's text, remains open and alive with the subtle optimism that the project of remaking yourself continues even after a book's end. It's not that Malin's year at the teachers' college culminates with a simple, satisfying resolution of her crisis. It's not that Malin transforms fully from a young woman wanting to annihilate her own will at the start of the book into a mature woman able to assert her will at the end of it. (Malin's transformative encounter with Siv, after all, is not the culmination of the novel, but rather its high point, located in the middle of the book, which then continues for several more sections.) Instead, Boye's narrative ends on a much more tenuous note, with Malin's radical choice to continue remaking herself in the world, despite all of its pleasures and horrors.

Malin's willingness to embrace the never-ending project of negotiating her boundaries offers an apt metaphor for the process of translation. I have thought a lot about the intimate connection between translation and the expressions of subjectivity in *Crisis*. Both reveal the fact that systems of meaning are never entirely fixed, the personal intertwines with things much larger, and that language is constantly

183

Amanda Doxtater

being adapted and reconsidered. Translation, like a self, never holds still; it is the antithesis of the idea of a fixed or essential I. Boye says as much with the opening scene of the novel, when Malin peers up at the images along the wall of the assembly hall and envisions the well of treasures that future generations will return to again and again. *Crisis* is one of these. It is my hope that this translation extends and accentuates Boye's remarkable creation of herself through text, by giving it new form, and new life, in a new language.

Acknowledgements

I am deeply indebted to the many people who have helped me with this project over the years. I am grateful to Tiina Nunnally for her early encouragement and wisdom, and to Sarah Death whose invaluable suggestions and meticulous attention to the manuscript in its late stages has improved it in ways that I could never have imagined possible. I'm very grateful also to Karen Emmerich for her generous and detailed reading of early drafts, but more generally for sharing her extensive experience teaching and practicing translation. Each encounter with these master translators has taught me so much.

Anna Jörngården, whose Swedish is so beautiful it brings tears to my eyes, read a version line by line with the Swedish. *Tack, min vän.* Kira Josefsson helped me untangle some of Boye's challenging passages. Thank you also to SOCE, who provided invaluable support as well as insight into how this book might be received by literary scholars unfamiliar with Boye. I have also benefitted greatly from discussions about queer kinship and translation with Maxine Savage. Thank you to Mark Safstrom for his insight into the theological and biblical references in the text, to Ursula Lindqvist for her suggestions for the snippets of poetry, and to Paul Norlén and Danielle Seid for their generous time in helping me edit the introduction. I'm grateful to my loving parents who brought me to Sweden in the first place and to my sister who inspires me every day. Watching her darling S. come into language has

Translator's Afterword

afforded me a new appreciation of the magic that translation is. A sincere thanks also to my dear friends the Werner-Hartman family who gave me my first copy of *Drabbad av renhet* so many years ago.

Ett stort tack to Lotta Gavel-Adams, who first introduced me to *Kris/Crisis*, and to Ia Dubois who discussed early sections of the translation with me. This project would not have been possible without the generous early support of the SWEA San Francisco Chapter which helped launch the project. And I'm deeply grateful to Barbro Osher, whose championing of Swedish culture in America is unparalleled. Her generous support has helped bring this project to completion. Last, but certainly not least, I would like to thank Norvik Press and particularly Claire Thomson for their otherworldly patience, understanding, and general brilliance.

Bibliography

Abenius, Margit. *Drabbad av renhet : en bok om Karin Boyes liv och diktning.* 2nd ed. Stockholm: Bonniers, 1951.

Domellöf, Gunilla. *I oss är en mångfald levande : Karin Boye som kritiker och prosamodernist.* PhD diss., Umeå Universitet, 1986. Universitetet i Umeå, 1986.

Doxtater, Amanda. 'Women Readers, Food and the Consumption of Text: Karin Boye's *Kris* and Monika Fagerholm's *Diva.*' *Gender, Power, Text: Nordic Culture in the Twentieth Century.* London: Norvik Press, 2004. pp. 125-137.

Enander, Crister. *Relief: författarporträtt.* Stockholm: Legus, 1995.

Jansson, Peter. *Själens krypta: en essä om Karin Boyes självbiografiska roman* Kris. Göteborg: Lindelöws Bokförlag, 2017.

Mesterton, Erik, Lars Fyhr, and Gunnar D Hansson. *Speglingar : essäer, brev, översättningar.* 2nd ed. Gråbo: Anthropos, 1985.

Rosenqvist, Barbro Gustafsson. *'Att skapa en ny värld': samhällssyn, kvinnosyn och djuppsykologi hos Karin Boye.* Stockholm: Carlsson, 1999.

Svedjedal, Johan. *Den nya dagen gryr: Karin Boyes författarliv.* Stockholm: Wahlström & Widstrand, 2017.

Svedjedal, Johan. *Spektrum 1931-1935: den svenska drömmen: tidskrift och förlag i 1930-talets kultur.* Stockholm: Wahlström & Widstrand, 2011.

SELMA LAGERLÖF
Mårbacka

(translated by Sarah Death)

The property of Mårbacka in Värmland was where Selma Lagerlöf grew up, immersed in a tradition of storytelling. Financial difficulties led to the loss of the house, but Lagerlöf was later able to buy it back, rebuild and make it the centre of her world. The book *Mårbacka*, the first part of a trilogy written in 1922-32, can be read as many different things: memoir, fictionalised autobiography, even part of Lagerlöf's myth-making about her own successful career as an author. It is part social and family history, part mischievous satire in the guise of innocent, first-person child narration, part declaration of filial love.

ISBN 9781909408296
UK £12.95
(Paperback, 270 pages)

VIGDIS HJORTH
A House in Norway

(translated by Charlotte Barslund)

A House in Norway tells the story of Alma, a divorced textile artist who makes a living from weaving standards for trade unions and marching bands. She lives alone in an old villa, and rents out an apartment in her house to supplement her income. She is overjoyed to be given a more creative assignment, to design a tapestry for an exhibition to celebrate the centenary of women's suffrage in Norway, but soon finds that it is a much more daunting task than she had anticipated. Meanwhile, a Polish family moves into her apartment, and their activities become a challenge to her unconscious assumptions and her self-image as a good feminist and an open-minded liberal. Is it possible to reconcile the desire to be tolerant and altruistic with the imperative need for creative and personal space?

ISBN 9781909408319
UK £11.95
(Paperback, 175 pages)

AMALIE SKRAM
Betrayed

(translated by Katherine Hanson and Judith Messick)

With high hopes, Captain Riber embarks with his young bride Aurora on a voyage to exotic destinations. But they are an ill-matched pair; her naive illusions are shattered by the realities of married life and the seediness of society in foreign ports, whilst his hopes of domestic bliss are frustrated by his wife's unhappiness. Life on board ship becomes a private hell, as Aurora's obsession with Riber's adventures as a carefree bachelor begins to undermine his sanity. Ultimately both are betrayed by a hypocritical society which imposes a warped view of sexuality on its most vulnerable members.

ISBN 9781909408494
UK £11.95
(Paperback, 136 pages)

CPSIA information can be obtained
at www.ICGtesting.com
Printed in the USA
BVHW030833011222
653197BV00012B/163